Ace reporter Kimberly Wells and cameraman Richard Adams are onto something really big . . .

THE CHINA SYNDROME

It means something very hot, very explosive. Something so big it could blow Southern California skyhigh!

THE CHINA SYNDROME

It's about power . . .
And it's about choices . . .
Between honesty and ambition . . .
Career and conscience . . .
Responsibility and profit . . .
Between the easy way out and the only way out . . .

THE CHINA SYNDROME

Only a handful of people know what it *really* means. But if Kimberly and Richard don't find out fast, it will be too late . . .

COLUMBIA PICTURES PRESENTS
A MICHAEL DOUGLAS/IPC FILMS PRODUCTION

A JAMES BRIDGES FILM

JACK LEMMON

JANE FONDA

MICHAEL DOUGLAS

THE CHINA SYNDROME

Written by
MIKE GRAY & T. S. COOK and JAMES BRIDGES

Associate Producer
JAMES NELSON

Executive Producer
BRUCE GILBERT

Producer
MICHAEL DOUGLAS

Directed by
JAMES BRIDGES

THE CHINA SYNDROME

Burton Wohl

Based on the Screenplay Written
by
Mike Gray & T. S. Cook
and
James Bridges

THE CHINA SYNDROME
A Bantam Book / March 1979

2nd printing
3rd printing

ISBN 0-553-13017-X

Published simultaneously in the United States and Canada

Bantam Books are published by Bantam Books, Inc. Its trademark, consisting of the words "Bantam Books" and the portrayal of a bantam is Registered in U.S. Patent and Trademark Office and in other countries. Marca Registrada. Bantam Books, Inc., 666 Fifth Avenue, New York, New York 10019.

PRINTED IN THE UNITED STATES OF AMERICA

THE
CHINA
SYNDROME

ONE

The air in the TV control room was neither rank nor sweet-smelling, cool nor warm, moving nor still. It was simply lifeless and in a way, dispirited. It had passed through too many ducts, too many fans and valves to retain that vital quality which we unconsciously associate with life.

On this particular afternoon, the monitors in KXLA's control room were reflecting Pete Martin's wide-eyed, toothy good looks from every possible camera angle.

Martin's chief gift was a never-flagging boyish enthusiasm, an enthusiasm which he had parlayed with a protean voice into a $175,000 per annum contract with a five-year option.

But it was not Martin's dazzling incisors that commanded the attention of the crew in the dimly lighted control room. To a man, they were peering into their screens to catch every little movement of Kimberly Wells, the most recent addition to Channel Three's news team.

Kimberly was being fed in from a remote pick-up at the rehearsal hall of The Live Wires, a singing telegram company staffed by eager young musical performers who were trying to survive in Hollywood without waiting tables and parking cars. Their little business, based on the gimmick of a surprise "live" delivery of a message for a special occasion, was enjoying more than modest success. In a town dominated by "show" business, a cute busty chorine in a hot pants version of a bellhop's uniform still managed to attract attention and earn spin-off jobs with one unexpected appearance. (A birthday telegram to Kimberly's boss Mac Churchill from a cohort at another station had prompted this little human interest piece. Mac couldn't wait for his old buddy to see this on the tube tonight. Mac was known for his one-upman ship.)

Kimberly was holding her own amid a special kind of bedlam. Technicians were swarming around her checking lights and mikes. With both impatience and humor she swatted the lingering hands of a sound man pinning an RF mike to her blouse.

"Studio B, this is remote," she said with a noticeable trace of urgency. An odd assortment of tackily costumed people drifted into the room.

A gawky bearded young man with a UCSB T-shirt showing under his gossamer "Swami" robes donned a pastel-blue turban and sat down in front of a set of bongo drums. A well-fed female in bangles and spangles was practicing some exotic movements that passed for belly dancing. On the sidelines, a young couple formally attired in tux and evening dress were vocalizing the opening bars of what sounded like opera. A station electrician rolled his eyes backward in mock revulsion.

"Hey, what's going on? Is anybody there? Mac, are you there?" Kimberly pleaded in a voice that sounded sultry when she slipped out of her professional demeanor.

"Mac, here," her boss answered absent-mindedly. "What's up?"

"We need at least five minutes before you hit us," she began. "Can you make it after the commercial?"

"Can't do it," he said flat out. "This is the last section."

"Can you at least give us two?"

Stopwatch in hand he answered, "We should be coming to you in forty seconds—"

"You can't," Kimberly panicked. "We don't have a cameraman."

"Where the hell is George?"

"He's taking a leak," she replied matter-of-factly. "What do you want me to tell you. He locked the camera down before he left. This is a two and one-half-minute spot and it isn't going to hold in a static shot."

Mac sighed with a decade of weariness in his voice and said to the director, "Give Pete the stretch. Remote's not ready."

Kimberly took advantage of the pause to spell out her plan. "I want to start it on a tight shot of me. Then after I introduce them, pull back wide."

"No problem. Just get George back." He added hastily, "And tell that belly dancer to keep it cool. I love her message but this is a *family* program. If she jiggles too much and pops out of that bikini top, we're in big trouble. This show is *live*."

"Oh, Mac." Kimberly sighed with a newly acquired weariness that came out of her own experience as a woman trying to operate professionally. The belly dancer (Kimberly knew from a preshow conversation) was a graduate student at UCLA and about to collect her master's degree in broadcasting. She wanted to be a television news producer. Hah, thought Kimberly, wait'll she applies to Mac for a job.

While Mac was busy finessing the details of a smooth delay, his boss, station manager Don Jacovich, and Jerry Faulks, the marketing consultant who had suggested Kimberly for the job, discussed the assets of their mutual choice.

Preening like a proud parent, Jerry congratulated himself. "She looks great. I knew it. Just knew it."

Jacovich concurred, "Our noon ratings are up half a point since she's come on."

"I know," Jerry said a bit smugly. "Our research showed she'd do well in the L.A. market. She was being wasted in Sacramento. This girl's got class—as well as a few more obvious assets. She could go all the way."

Jacovich agreed but inwardly felt a tinge of resentment. "All the way" meant network, meant New York. If she was that good, he'd only be able to hold onto her for a year or so. He'd cautiously signed her for only a year, with an option for another. Maybe he'd better renegotiate now. But, hell, you can't hold a hot one with an ironclad contract. Better, he thought, he'd really use her, bolster his ratings, exploit her appeal, and eventually overexpose her. A bird in hand.

Almost reading his mind, Jerry asked, "What do you think of the way she dresses?"

"Fine, fine," Jacovich nodded. Personally, he liked the way she looked, spoke, read copy, liked everything about her except that sometimes she got too serious.

"Clothes could be sexier, I suppose," Jerry admitted. "She sort of plays down her body but maybe she's right. The effect in the end is very provocative because she never flashes any skin or wears clingy stuff. Keeps 'em panting without offending the wives."

"Right," Jacovich agreed. "We're using her on the 'Evening News' and highlighting her on the 'Live at Noon' show. Our weakness was daytime. I don't want a knockout like Kimberly intimidating the housefraus."

"Exactly," Jerry said, adding, "when it comes right down to it, that hair is her on-camera I.D. Nobody in the business has hair like that. It's dynamite."

"You don't think it's a bit much, then?" asked Jacovich conservatively.

"Hell, no," Jerry countered. "Maybe shorter. Not too much, *men* like long hair on their women. Would she cut it a little?"

"She'll do anything we say," Jacovich said emphatically. "She wants to make it. She's really serious about her work."

"She seeing anyone from the station?" Jerry asked unexpectedly.

"I really don't get involved with the private

lives of my staff," Jacovich answered icily.

"Just wondering," mumbled Jerry as they both turned to watch Kimberly run her fingers through her long red hair, moisten her lips with her tongue, and begin her on-camera dialogue.

"What did you do the last time someone had a birthday? Did you send a card, candy, or perhaps flowers? Boring, huh? How about something a bit more imaginative? Here's one idea that's taking L.A. by storm."

Beside her, a uniformed fellow burst on the scene singing a Happy Birthday message. As he danced off-camera the opera duet descended on Kimberly, and she continued, "There's one for every occasion. Maybe it's your parents who are celebrating their fiftieth wedding anniversary and you'd like to send them an Operagram . . .

"Or maybe you have a message that words cannot express . . ." the belly dancer and her accompanist slithered onto the scene.

In the control room, Mac was pleased with her smooth delivery. It had just the ideal combination of enthusiasm and amused condescension that newspeople acquired after years of reading ludicrous copy. An assistant waved a telephone at him and signaled to pick-up. He grabbed the phone, keeping an eye on the monitor which featured a close-up of the nubile belly dancer doing her thing. Mac answered the voice on the phone in a distracted way; he nodded while keeping his finger poised on a button that would punch the action onto another camera if the belly dancer got out of hand, or out of bra, as the case might be.

"Uh, who? Yeah. That's right. She was the one who suggested it for a feature. She can handle it all right. Tell him it's on and we'll get back to him if there's any hitch. I'm sure we can fit it in this afternoon."

Mac turned back to glance at Jerry and found him engrossed in the tiny screen. Kimberly's hooked her own Pygmalion, Mac thought to himself. And this is a rating point that counts.

"That's a bellygram and words cannot express that," she concluded. "This is Kimberly Wells, 'Live at Noon.' "

"That's it kiddies," a technician called, yanking arcs and audio equipment out of their sockets with more speed than the set-up. "We're off the air."

"Hey, Kimberly, schedule change," the assistant director Tom called. "They just set another assignment for this afternoon."

"I don't believe it. Just for once, I'd like to get through a whole day, even a whole morning, without having the rug yanked out."

"Hey, lady, I didn't do nothin'. It's Mac. He just got a call from that nuke plant. What's it called, Ventana? We're clear to go over there this afternoon and make some movies."

"Ventana? Really? Great. I'd just about given up on them. I think I first called them about a month ago. Who've we got for a crew?"

"Richard and Hector."

"Richard! Terrific. They did the other segments. At least we'll have continuity."

"And trouble. Your ex-bomb thrower had better be on his best behavior."

"Richard? Richard," she protested, "is a political activist, not a bomb thrower."

"Same difference. Listen, there's a McDonald's out on the highway about three miles before you get to the plant. They'll be waiting for you at 1:00 and you're supposed to be out there between one and two. Now don't shack up in any motels along the way. . . ."

"You really are a disgusting, stone-age flathead of a male chauvinist pig."

"You think that's something," Tom said, taking her microphone from her, "wait'll you see me tap dance. Everybody back on the bus. Jimmie? Lee? Leave them naked ladies alone, you'll get sand on your hands."

Kimberly eased herself into the front seat of the truck. There was, as there is in every mini-society, a pecking order in the group, and it was generally recognized that the newscaster, was accorded top position in that order, even though he or she was not able to plug in a jack or start up a spool of tape or turn on a light switch, and was practically useless for any human activity other than reading the news. It wasn't much, Kimberly thought, but it did give her the time to repair her make-up, compose her thoughts for the next gig and even get in a nap once in a while.

She felt good to be sitting in this truck, with these guys, barreling along the Pacific Coast highway. She had wanted to be where she was, had wanted it for a long time, schemed and fought and worked for it, and she wasn't about to have late-blooming remorse. Ever since college she wanted to do something more with herself than walk up and down in front of jittery, horny, or arrogant fashion photographers wearing clothes that she couldn't afford. She'd done that and all it had gotten her was a year and a half in analysis —which she could not afford—and a husband, ditto. The husband did have one advantage, however. As an advertising executive, bent on destroying himself and everyone around him, he knew several indestructible people, some of whom turned out to be in TV. It was to one of these, a TV news director, that Kimberly repaired when her erstwhile husband strayed from the marital nest.

From a philandering husband to a TV news director. He was kindly, absent-minded, undemanding and saw to it that she got a job in the news room. Little by little, she worked her way up and out. Up the ladder and out of the office staff until she finally landed a spot on the news team in Sacramento. It took her a little more than a year and a half but she was finally spotted by a marketing consultant scouting fresh blood for the anemically rated KXLA. They broke her contract in one day and she was on a plane to L.A. by the weekend.

And not the least bit sorry. Not that Los Angeles was Kimberly's idea of nirvana. In truth, she really didn't have an idea of nirvana. Two weeks in Montego Bay seemed like a pleasant notion, depending on who you were with.

But what she really wanted and wanted very deeply, was to get to New York and be nothing less than anchor person on her very own show. If Barbara could parlay a lisp and a lot of chutzpah into a million bucks a year, then she, Kimberly Wells, could do the same. She didn't have the lisp, but she had no shortage of whatever it was that came out as chutzpah, call it drive, determination, or just plain ambition.

Having completed her make-up, along with a plastic cup of lukewarm coffee, she gave herself up, as she sometimes did, to free-floating fantasies about "the good life in New York." It started out with a suite—no, a floor—at the Carlyle, a sherry and a shaggy mongrel dog waiting to greet her when she came in from her own network news show or acclaimed one-hour special on the new Pope or Muhammed Ali. There was a man somewhere around the edges of this fantasy, she was sure of that. But she wasn't sure what he looked like or even if he would be important. When she came right down to it, there wasn't a man, not anywhere she looked, who seemed to belong in her fantasy future. Maybe someday he'd come along, she thought, and comforted herself with the additional thought that, even if he didn't come along, what the hell. This was a whole new age, and a woman didn't need a man to complete her existence. A thorough professional, she fell into a doze when the van hit the freeway. A special kind of doze. It didn't muss her hair or smudge her make-up. Kimberly Wells was ready to come out of the slot at running speed.

She had no trouble spotting her crew when the van let her off at McDonald's. Richard Adams, an intense young man with disorderly hair and a beard to match, sat at the wheel of a battered Ford Bronco. The 4-wheel drive looked as if it had spent the last three years submerged up to the floorboards in a salt marsh, being roosted on by sea gulls. It was half rusted away, battle scarred, salt encrusted, mouse infested, and it drove, because of a blown-out engine, like a shutter-banging bomb.

Next to Adams sat Hector Salas, a chunky, smooth-faced chicano with shoulders the size and shape of a truck radiator. Salas's manner was as amiable as his expression, which was a good thing on the whole, because a combination of all those muscles and bad temper would be dangerous to public order. Kimberly knew Salas to be an excellent sound man but she didn't know him well.

Adams, on the other hand, was someone she'd known awhile. They'd met when she was doing commercials, before she cared about being something more than just another pretty face. Richard wasn't quite used to the ambitious change in Kimberly. It amused him. She was becoming a real proponent of the Establishment. He, on the other hand, was using the Establishment for a fast buck and no qualms about it. Richard was a regular organizer of civil rights marches, Viet Nam protest marches, free speech movements, campus disturbances, Greenpeace demonstrations, liberation movements of every kind and of every persuasion. Adams was not merely a cause-joiner, he was a riot-inciter, flame-fanner, activist, agit-prop, and establishment-critic. His head had more scars from police clubs, his dossier had more minor arrests on misdemeanor charges, his pad had housed more dissident refugees than Abbie Hoffman. Adams hung in there, doing his gigs as a free-lance cameraman—gigs that weren't hard to come by because there wasn't another cameraman in Southern California who could set up a shot as quickly and capture it as well—while waiting for the right cause to come along.

He took one look as Kimberly got out of the van and averted his gaze. She wasn't the right cause at all. They'd had a little waltz together when she first came to town. They'd spent a little time, smoked a little, danced a little, laid back a little wine together and that was about as far as it ever got. Richard wasn't about to settle for a vine-clad duplex with roses hanging over the Mercedes. And Kimberly wasn't about to lose her hard-won status by shuffling up Laurel Canyon in a granny dress and bare feet after a spaced-out morning dozing over Bill Baker's bean sprouts.

"You were born a blood donor," she'd told Richard at the time of their parting.

"And you're a corporate management commando," he'd thrust back.

Both were partly right, both partly wrong. And neither had ever quite forgotten that—if only for a short time—something had happened between them something that had given both an inner warmth.

'Hi, guys," Kimberly greeted them, "how much time do we have to get there?"

"Hey, wha' you say, mama," Hector grinned, "you lookin' pretty good, like you bought your clo's from Anita Bryant."

"We've been poisoning ourselves eating junk food, waiting for you," Adams said grumpily. "I mean, imagine getting past Lester Maddox and his axe handles, only to be done in by a Big Mac or an Egg McMuffin."

"You're looking chipper as usual, Richard," Kimberly said good-naturedly. "Your dialogue hasn't improved but the shirt is reasonably clean. I'm glad at least that you thought to wear a shirt."

"Shirt," Richard growled, slamming the Bronco in gear and screaming backward out of the parking lot, "we ought to be wearing shrouds. Morning costumes. Do you know what this whole thing is about? Have you any idea what's going down?"

Kimberly swallowed a couple of times before answering. It didn't do to rise directly to Richard's bait because he always had something in his sock, something to club you with when you engaged his first premise.

"What's going down," she said, trying to shout into the slip-stream, "is that we're going to do a standard interview with the PR honcho of a nuclear generating plant. Now this whole thing could just turn out to be white bread or it could come out interesting, depending on what we get into."

"What we get into!" Richard snorted and jabbed Salas with his elbow. "Did you hear that? What do you think we're going to get *into*, chickie? What do you think the front office man is going to *let* us get into? You think they're going to take us down into the pickle works, where we can photograph the whole scam? You think they're going to let us really see anything? Like where they bury the shit they can't burn off?"

"Goddam it, Richard!" Kimberly lost her temper despite herself. "It's an assignment, not a cause. Okay? You take the gig, you shut up and do the job. I'll ask the questions. And if I don't ask the questions *you* want answered, mail them in. You got that?"

Richard answered by slumping down in his seat and blowing air out of puffed cheeks. Even an activist needs to live and he was, as usual, behind in his rent, behind in just about everything else. It even occurred to him that Hector Salas had to spring for the garbage they'd been eating. It also occurred to him that he'd better shut up and drive.

"Isn't there someway you can load up this jeep so that I don't get a camera case in my neck?" Kimberly shouted at him.

Richard didn't answer. A buck is a buck is a buck, he told himself, and kept right on driving.

Even before they got into a slow-speed area, the Ventana Nuclear Power Plant was impressive enough to lift Richard's foot off the accelerator. A large, bullet-shaped dome rose up over a huge block structure, towering some fifteen stories above the surrounding sand and chaparral. All of the connecting buildings were massive and windowless, so that the initial impression of this huge establishment was one of silence. Eerie, mysterious silence. A few parked cars were baking out in the lot. There were no guards visible, no traffic, no vehicles moving back and forth inside the barbed-wire-topped fences. It was both awesome and spooky to come upon something so vast, so potent, and to encounter nothing but the sighing of wind from the surrounding desert, a sigh which only emphasized the deep, even ominous silence.

Richard pulled to a stop and reached under Kimberly's legs for his camera, even as she was trying to scramble out of the jeep.

A few minutes later, with almost no exchange among the three of them, Kimberly was facing Richard's camera, her back to the huge nuclear generating plant, Hector Salas's recorder turning over silently in the back of the jeep.

"Hello," Kimberly said, looking into the camera. "This is Kimberly Wells and I'm standing just outside the grounds of the Ventana Nuclear Power Plant, owned and operated by California Gas and Electric. The plant is just behind me. That huge dome you see is called the Containment, and houses the nuclear fuel. In this section of our continuing look at Energy in California, Yesterday, Today and Tomorrow, we will focus on nuclear energy, that almost magical transformation of matter into energy that, the experts tell us, is our best shot at energy selfish sufficience—oh, shit!"

"Cut!" Hector called.

"Whatsa matter?" Richard wanted to know.

"She said selfish," Hector said. "Selfish sufficiency instead of self-sufficiency."

"So who's listening?"

"Just a minute," Kimberly dug into her bag and pulled out a script. "Give me a cigarette, will you, Richard. I know, I know, I gave it up. But this is show biz and it makes me nervous." Her features softened briefly as he lighted a cigarette and handed it to her. Then she frowned over her script again.

"Self-sufficiency, there it is. Self—self—self. Self sufish. Self suffish. Self suffishin. Self suffishincy. Self sufficiency. Okay, let's roll 'em one more time."

Hector Salas muttered into his mike. "Kimberly Wells, Energy special, Ventana Nuclear Plant, take two . . ."

"Hello," Kimberly said, smiling once more into the camera. "I'm Kimberly Wells and I'm here at the . . ."

This time it went off without a hitch.

While they were returning their equipment to the jeep, a little white Pinto came out of the chain link gate in front of the plant and drove swiftly to where they stood. A pleasant-looking man in his early forties, with a practiced smile and a professionally laid-back manner, greeted them from the driver's seat.

"Hi, KXLA news team? Kimberly Wells? I'm Bill Gibson, public information director for Ventana."

"Public information!" Richard snorted under his breath to Hector. "El flack-o. PR guys, the pits!"

"Shut up, Richard," Kimberly warned in an undertone.

Gibson ambled over, smiling, smoothing his hair. "Looks like you've got a perfect day for your outdoor stuff."

"I hope you didn't mind," Kimberly said. "I thought we'd pick up a master shot out here before going into the plant. The light's awfully good now and we might not have enough light for a good daytime shot when we come out."

"Good thinking. We'd prefer people to get a good clear look in bright sunshine. Makes it all seem more real, less sci-fi-ish."

Richard guffawed. "Sy Fyish! Say, does he work here? I haven't seen him—"

Kimberly broke in quickly. "Uh, this is Richard Adams, camera and stand-up comic, and Hector Salas, audio."

"Hiya, fellas," Gibson said easily. "Glad you could make it out here. Why don't you put all your gear in the back of my car and I'll drive you into the plant."

"Whatsamatter, my car bad for the neighborhood?" Adams said. He was smiling. Mirthlessly.

"Hell, no." Gibson gestured. "Just that we've got pretty tight security—I'm sure you can appreciate that, Kimberly—and my car has been checked and re-checked. It'll just save time if they don't have to search your car."

"Oh, okay, man, no sweat. I've got a ki of hash in the tool box and I'd just as soon the guards didn't flash on that. And Hector here never travels without his mayonnaise jar full of reds. I try to tell him—"

"Uh, Richard—" Kimberly's voice carried a warning note.

"I thought we'd talk for a little bit," Bill Gibson said. "You tell me what you'd like to get. I'll tell you some things you might want to shoot that you probably don't even know about and also some stuff that you can't shoot. O.K.?"

"Sounds good to me," Kimberly said. "We're green. You fill us in and then we'll see what we can put together."

"Fine," Gibson said, opening the doors of his car. "Uh, Adams, why don't you sit up front so that the guard can take a look at your camera and Kimberly, if you and Salas would sit in back . . ."

Sharp, Kimberly thought. Not only did he get the names right the first time, he put her a touch off-balance by stashing her in the back seat. This dude, she told herself, was no glad-handing Lions Club publicity chairman.

At the gate, a smartly uniformed, smiling, but no-nonsense guard firmly insisted on examining the camera.

"Hey, don't even think about opening that box, man," Adams said.

"Just need to X-ray it, sir. Won't take a moment."

"But there's raw film in there. Jesus Christ!" Adams wheeled to face Gibson.

"Uh, Chuck," Gibson said, "okay if I personally vouch for the camera? These people are a TV news team and were approved by upstairs."

"Okay, Mr. Gibson, if you'll just sign this form, I'll let the camera inside in your custody."

"Thanks. Uh—excuse me, Kimberly? Adams? Salas? You do have some form of ID?"

"Of course," Kimberly said, "but you don't think we'd come out here in this heat with audio and video equipment unless we—"

"Mind showing me your ID?"

Kimberly's smile faded The man was serious. "Oh—well, sure. Here's my—" she hunted around in her purse "—um, here it is. Studio pass."

"Good," Gibson smiled, handing it back to her.

He turned to face Adams and Salas, both of whom gave Kimberly a questioning look. "Go ahead," she said.

Then, dutifully, they came up with their ID cards.

"Thanks folks," Gibson said, after he'd seen all their cards. He casually saluted the guard and drove slowly toward a parking area near the administration building. "I'm sorry about the red tape," he added, "but on the other hand, I wouldn't think you'd want it any other way. We're super-cautious, about security, engineering, everything. We have to be. Since I'm signing as responsible party for the camera equipment, I want to be darned sure I know who I'm dealing with."

"I think you make a good point, Mr. Gibson, and I may want to cover that in our show."

"You can call me Bill—it'll be easier in the long run."

"And you can call me Richard. Not Dick, Promise?"

"Promise," Gibson grinned. It was clear that no amount of needling was going to wear down his even temper and Adams found this depressing. There was nothing that frustrated him more than losing an arm-wrestling match because his opposite number wouldn't take his hands out of his pockets.

"Now, first we have to go through the security gate—through those glass doors. The guards will check you out, just the way they do in airports."

"Boy, Hector, I hope you didn't bring those dumb grenades with you again."

"Hey, no way, man. Just a couple molotovs—the machine don't groove on glass, you know."

"They're always a handful," Kimberly said, "until they get through the third grade. Once they're really good at sight-reading—"

Gibson laughed and then dumped all of his change, keys and other metal objects into a plastic tray. The armed and uniformed guard took the tray, scrutinized it briefly, then motioned Gibson to pass by the metal detector. Once past that, another guard carefully patted Gibson's body down.

"Uh, Kimberly, if you'd go through that aisle . . ." Gibson motioned to an adjacent aisle where a uniformed female guard waited at the other end "A body search is mandatory."

"Fine with me, but couldn't I have a drink first?"

"Now who's being smart-ass," Adams growled. "Go through the gate, lady, and let Butchy there cop a feel. Hector, what do you say we forget the whole gig and go search each other. I mean really search and probe and—"

"Down, man, they're waiting for you."

Kimberly started to pass the metal detector but was stopped by a high-pitched whine. "Now, what the—I took off just about everything I could—"

"Any metal will do it," the female guard said pleasantly. "Bracelet, garters, safety pins."

"Safety pins! I promised my mother I'd never go—I know! I've got a spare dime in my pocket."

"If you'll just step in here, Miss, so we can have a look."

"But it's just a thin dime. See?"

"In here," the guard repeated, holding open a door to a little brightly lighted cubicle. "Won't take a second."

"Richard," Kimberly said, "if anything happens, be sure to put the cover on my terrarium."

Adams was too busy to reply. One by one, the guards were going over the bits and pieces of his equipment. And while they were examining his gear, another guard was giving him a professional body search.

"Boy, you guys don't leave anything to chance, do you?" Adams remarked, obviously impressed by their thoroughness.

"That's our business, sir, security."

"That's good," Adams circled his thumb and forefinger in a sign of approval. "Because when you've got this kind of a store, somebody had better be watching it."

The briefing with Gibson took place in his pleasant, well-lighted but windowless office and was straightforward and business-like. He briefly outlined the main features of the plant, told them what they could see and what they could not. "For safety reasons, primarily," he explained. "Our insurance policy doesn't cover non-authorized personnel in certain areas. Not so much a matter of radiation, although there are areas where that is naturally a hazard, but because of heavy equipment, excess heat, or just the simple danger of slipping and falling off a metal ladder. A good deal of our operation is no different from any other heavy industry and presupposes the usual safeguards."

"Well," Kimberly said, "in checking over my notes, I'd say you're doing right well by us. I didn't think we'd get to shoot the reactor core. For goodness sake, who'd want to?"

"Me, I'd want to," Richard said. "Ever since I was a little kid, I've wanted to see one of those things."

"And get turned into a taco? Who needs it?" Kimberly said.

"Hector. Hector turns into a taco. Me, I turn into an Egg McMuffin. Seriously, folks—"

"Yeah, I sure wish—"

"O.K.," Richard said, swinging his camera up on his shoulder. "Why don't we do a little footage on this plant model, with you and Gibson talking, Kimberly. It'll give us a sort of a lead-in, we might want to edit it down later, but—"

"I think you're right. This model is really very visual and we've got a lot of explaining to do. The general public doesn't know beans about all this stuff."

"Our number-one job," Gibson said. "Educating the public. Education is the only way through all the fear and hysteria"

"Maybe the more we know, the more we ought to be afraid, Mr. Gibson," Adams said.

"And maybe you will just start unwinding film and let me do the interview, huh, Richard, bubbie?" Kimberly cut in.

"Yeah, go. Take one." Adams switched on a powerful light mounted on a tripod, handed Kimberly a microphone and put his eye to the view-finder.

"Kimberly Wells. I'm sitting here in the conference room of the Ventana Nuclear Power Plant with William Gibson, public relations director for California Gas and Electric."

"I'd prefer public information director, Kimberly, if you don't mind."

"Oh, sure. Let's do that over, Richard." She repeated her opening remarks exactly and corrected his title. "And now, Mr. Gibson—"

"Please call me Bill, Kimberly."

Kimberly smiled and continued smoothly. "Bill Gibson is going to tell us just how this amazing plant works."

"I'll try to make it simple because it really is simple—in principle, that is. The technology is complicated, of course, but the basic operation is really no different from any other power plant. This is a nuclear plant designed to manufacture electricity. That's been done for many years in this country, using coal or oil, natural gas, water power. But here, in order to make electricity we use uranium for our fuel. Now, this model that I'm standing next to will show you how we do it. Uh—" Gibson paused and looked up.

"Do you want to come in closer on this model, or is it all right from where you're standing?"

"No, no, that's fine. I'm still rolling and I've got it all in the picture. Just keep on doing what you were doing."

"How about me, Richard?" Kimberly asked. "Am I in the shot or is it a single?"

"Single on Gibson. I'll swing back to you in a minute for a reverse. Go on, kids, the camera's wailing."

"This," Gibson said, taking a small pellet out of his pocket, "is a pellet of simulated uranium, the same size, color and weight of the actual uranium pellet that is placed in our fuel rods. Naturally, this is plastic, one doesn't carry highly radioactive material around in his trousers pocket. Now, there are exactly 20,000,000 of these uranium pellets inside stainless steel rods which make up the reactor vessel or core. That's this object here on the model. The core is totally covered by water which is used to cool it. In addition to these fuel rods, there is also another set of stainless steel rods called control rods. And these rods do actually control the nuclear reaction. They speed it up or slow it down. What happens is, when the core is activated, put on line, as we call it, the nuclear fuel begins a chain reaction, resulting in a tremendous amount of heat. As the heat builds, the temperature is controlled by the movement of the control rods. But the object is: to use the heat to boil the water to make the steam which turns the turbine, which turns the electric generator, which makes the electricity—to power your TV or make your toast or whatever. And it's all as simple as that." Gibson smiled and looked up.

"Thank you," Kimberly smiled, "for a useful introduction." She looked at Richard. "Is that O.K., or do you want more?"

"That's great," Richard said. "Let me just move this light around so we can get your reverse. Hey baby, stick out your can, heah come de reversal ma'an." He sang to himself as he moved, underscoring his more cheerful mood.

Gibson moved away. "Uh, Kimberly, if you don't need me for a couple of minutes, I've a few things to clear up in my office. I'll be back with some hard hats."

"Good. Oh, Bill—not red. Please."

"White O.K.?"

"Super."

"Make mine strawberry ripple," Richard said, squinting into his camera and gesturing to Kimberly. "O.K., doll, same position as before, I'm doing your reaction shot. Keep your eyes on the model."

"Yeah, O.K. it's just this eye-liner." Kimberly was peering at her eye in her compact mirror.

"Oh, for Christ's sake. Is this the news or are we doing a lounge act at Vegas? Do we have to go on with this cosmetic shit?"

"You're damned right we do," Kimberly said, coolly, not taking her eyes off the mirror and carefully touching up a smudge. "So just buzz off and let me get my image together."

"Image," Richard sighed. "Your image is fantastic. Believe me, if I throw any more shadow underneath your tits, you'll look like Wonder Woman. Will you put away the garbage, Kimberly—O.K., O.K., here we go. Rolling. That's good. You're listening to Gibson. Beautiful. Beautiful. Yeah, yeah, listening, nodding, agreeing, while he cons the shit out of you and all the great unwashed out there who are paying for this shit and that's good, nodding, yeah, listening—and all the unborn kids who are going to grow up with little hands like hamsters and three nostrils, on account of this shit in the atmosphere, yeah, really interesting. I can see he turns you on, beautiful, right? What we have here is the future death of the whole world and you're nodding and agreeing, and what the fuck are they going to do with the waste products, keep it underwater for twenty five thousand years? Are you ready for—"

Gibson returned, carrying a cluster of plastic hard hats. "O.K., Richard," Kimberly called out, a trifle sharply, "that's enough. I think we've covered it."

"Hey, wait, we don't have enough cut-aways

yet," Richard objected, continuing to track her with the camera, "hey, stay in the light, goddamnit."

"I said that's enough!" Kimberly's voice turned steely.

"Yeah, right, wrapping it up. We'll get some more later."

"You folks ready?" Gibson handed out the hats. "One size fits all. There's an elastic band inside."

"I really like to wear these things," Hector said, "because the soft spot on my skull never closed up since I was a baby. That's one reason why I never get inside a Volkswagen."

"Come on," Richard said. "You wanna eat popcorn and cheeseburgers and malts, that'll harden your damn head for you."

"We eat jalapeno peppers. Sheee!"

"God!" Kimberly moaned. "This undergraduate clowning. What *is* it with you two? Are you trying to develop a sitcom? Will you please do it on your own time?"

"Sure, teach," Richard grinned, "you just point us at the action and we'll film it. Hey, Gibson, did you say we could photograph inside the containment area?"

"Afraid not, not while the plant's on-line. Operating, that is. I think I'd better lead the way. So if you'll just follow me . . ." He headed through the door.

Just before leaving the room, Richard snatched up the plastic "uranium" pellet and popped it between his teeth. "Don't touch me," he whispered fiercely to Kimberly. "I'll turn you into an electric tooth-brush."

"Richard," Kimberly muttered between clenched teeth. "If you blow this gig for me, you son of a bitch, I will kill you. Do you understand, you childish, self-indulgent, son of a bitch."

"Pamela!" Richard clowned. "I never dreamed you cared. Really cared."

She elbowed him in the stomach. "And that," she muttered, "is just for openers."

They followed Gibson down long, utterly antiseptic corridors, well-lit but windowless. It was an eerie feeling, somehow charged with energy, mystery. And yes, Kimberly thought, even danger.

At a certain point, Gibson held up a hand and the little caravan stopped. He was about to open a very large, very heavy metal door marked Closed To Unauthorized Personnel, and ornamented with the three-bladed yellow and magenta sticker, the emblem of the nuclear age, the radiation warning sign.

"This is the turbine room," Gibson said. He addressed Richard. "You can shoot anything you want from the positions that I take you to. But don't try to get any closer unless you check with me, O.K?"

They filed in. And were almost knocked flat by the volume of engine sound. The turbines, two-hundred-feet-long, spun in their vast steel cocoons like awakening wasps, emitting a growling whine that not only savaged the ear, but chilled the heart as well. Kimberly shuddered and felt a wave of vertigo, which caused her to go pale and grip the guard rail for support.

Gibson shouted something to her which she did not at first understand. "Terrifying, isn't it?" he repeated, smiling reassurance.

She nodded, fearful of opening her mouth, aware that nausea was growing inside her. There was something fascinating about being close to the source of so much power but there was something sickening about it as well. She was, she realized, close to an immense source of death, as well as to a source of life. She wanted desperately to escape, to burst into calm and fresh air and sunshine; but she was also enough of the professional to force back her fears, ignore the queasy sensation just behind her palate and get her job done.

Everywhere there were massive ducts and tubes, painted in bright colors to indicate their function, huge valve handles as large as basketball hoops, banks of meters and dials and groups of auxiliary machines—pumps, compressors, blowers. Many of these machines gave off their own subsidiary noises and over the entire room, as large as a dirigible hangar, there hung an invisible but distinctive atmosphere of ozone—the smell of air altered by electro-magnetic activity.

Richard seemed energized by the unfamiliar environment, checking his light meter, focusing his camera, crouching, bobbing, zooming in and out. Hector kept pace with him, following Richard with the sound boom, adjusting the balance on his tape recorder, checking the quality of the sound on each take.

It took Kimberly a while before she recovered sufficiently for her to frame questions. Looking down at her hand still gripping the guard rail, she noticed that her knuckles were white. Gibson caught her glance. "Kinda gets to you, doesn't it?"

"Sure does," she smiled weakly.

"We don't bring school children in here—not the earliest grades, that is. Too frightening. But this is no different from any big electrical plant anywhere. Just big turbines, that's all. But at first, they scare the hell out of you."

"How old is this plant?"

"We became operational, about four years ago. But it took nearly twelve years to build. When I say build, you understand: I mean build and install and test—very carefully. One step at a time. And each step has to be approved by the nuclear regulating people. So it's a lengthy process. As, I'm sure you'll agree, it should be. Oh, by the way, I'll give you a fact sheet before you leave so that you can use it when you put your story together. It'll give you the answers to a lot of the questions you'll be asking right now. But go ahead and ask."

"O.K.," Kimberly said, "I think Richard's got enough footage in here. Is there somewhere we can go—like outside, where we don't have to shout at each other?"

"Sure," Gibson smiled. He pointed to a door and touched her arm. The others followed.

Once outside, Kimberly felt an immense sense of relief; the immersion in that tremendous volume of sound had been enervating.

"Haven't you people got another plant not very far from here that you're setting up?" Richard asked.

"Yes," Gibson said, "we're hoping to be licensing our Point Conception works in a few weeks. There was some talk of my going over there for the start-up but that's not settled yet."

"That's right," Kimberly said, remembering, "those hearings are in progress now, aren't they? In fact, I think I saw something on the schedule about our covering them."

"I hope you do," Gibson said. "It'll be quite an education for you. Those things get really gritty. I mean, challenging. Nothing is taken for granted. Not just the kind of shoe soles the workmen are going to wear, but the laces too! They really get into details."

"Well," Kimberly said, "it's not as if this were just another potato chip factory. This affects a lot of people."

"That's right. If all goes well, that plant should go on-line some time late in 1979. What that means is, these two plants combined, will produce more power than Hoover Dam and Grand Coulee Dam, *combined*. That's a lotta power."

Kimberly scribbled some notes in a small pad which she kept in her hand as they walked down the spotless corridor. A distinguished-looking man came abreast of them and smiled briefly at Gibson. He was in his early fifties, Kimberly thought. Vigorous. Well-tanned. The kind of man who would be hard to beat at tennis.

"How are you, Bill?"

"Hi, Herman—uh, got a minute?" Gibson stopped the man by touching his arm. "This is

Kimberly Wells, Richard Adams, Hector Salas. KXLA news team."

"Oh, yes. Herman De Young," the man said.

"Plant manager," Gibson said, "our fearless leader."

"I heard you folks were coming out," De Young said, as he shook hands. "Bill told me about it a month ago. Sorry it took so long to get your clearances."

"Clearances!" Richard echoed.

"FBI," Gibson said easily. "Well, the normal procedure, I think, is through AEC and from them to FBI and I don't really know who-all. My secretary knows more about all that than I do."

"You mean to say the FBI cleared *me!*" Richard seemed incredulous. He grinned at Hector and then at Kimberly.

"If they hadn't," De Young said, "you couldn't get through those gates."

"I don't believe it," Richard said. "After all the marches I've been in. Hell, I got busted right in front of the Lincoln Memorial. I thought those guys had a file on me a foot thick."

Gibson laughed. "They probably do but who knows, maybe it's full of valentines. One thing I do know, they wouldn't have O.K.'d you if they didn't think you were clean."

"I can't get over it." Richard continued to shake his head. "What does a guy have to do to be marked really lousy? Paint a moustache on Anita Bryant?"

"Actually, Richard's just a clean-cut American kid, Mr. De Young," Kimberly said. "He just hates to admit that he's a member of 4-H and writes every week to his mother."

De Young laughed lightly. "Well, I hope you folks get what you want. Bill knows as much about this operation as anybody here. We're happy to have you aboard."

"And we're happy to *be* aboard, sir," Richard said, smiling and making a little mock salute. Then he went whistling down the corridor.

"Miss Wells," De Young said, "anything I can do for you . . ."

"Thank you," Kimberly smiled, shaking his hand.

When they were walking down the corridor again, Gibson nodded at Richard Adams.

"Are you two a regular team?"

"Not exactly," Kimberly said. "We used to work together in commercials."

"Oh, you're an actress then?"

"No. I was just doing production work. And Richard was a free-lance cameraman. Still is, for that matter."

"Very free, I should think," Gibson said. Kimberly glanced at him but saw that he meant it without malice. She smiled. "Very free, very independent. And very good, too."

They drew abreast of Richard and Hector and were about to pass through another door when Richard drew back his lips, revealing the "uranium pellet" clenched between his teeth.

"I am going to disstroy ziss antire eenstallation onless you giff me ze formula for your magnetic Tootsie Roll!" He snarled.

"Oh, Richard!" Kimberly broke up in spite

of herself. "You dummy! You look like a chow dog!"

"A *what?*"

"Your tongue is all black. The color's come off. You're contaminated."

"Oh, my God," Richard screamed, yanking the pellet out of his mouth. "I thought it was plastic."

"It was," Gibson grinned. "But I palmed it. What you've got in your mouth is a licorice jelly bean. One of the engineers thought it up as a gag and we sometimes pull it on visitors."

"A radioactive jelly bean!" Richard chortled "Brought by a nuclear Easter bunny!" He followed the others into an elevator. They ascended two floors and emerged onto a corridor exactly like the one below. This one was much quieter, however, with only the faintest trace of engine vibration.

"And this," Gibson said, ushering them into a glass-walled balcony, "is the visitor's gallery. And what you're looking down on is our control room."

"Holy—" Richard's comment faded to soundlessness.

Immediately below them was a large, brightly lit room with a uniformed and armed guard sitting at a table just in front of the entrance. On all four sides of the room were banks of consoles, each containing dozens of electric switches. Above these were lighted banks of gauges and signals, some with numbers flashing on and off, others with colored lights, still others with dials and oscilloscopes. Along the walls, computer printouts poured out reams of paper into baskets. The room looked like a combination of a submarine bridge, aircraft cockpit and missile control center.

Kimberly looked at Gibson. "Wow!" she said. "I've never seen anything like it. My God—the cost of setting up this room alone . . ."

Gibson nodded. "This is the nerve center. The brain, actually. Impulses come in and signals are sent out. In some areas there are not one or two, but half a dozen back-up systems. And the whole thing is bullet-proof, sound-proof, attack-proof."

"I can see why," Richard said. "A terrorist in there could blackmail the hell out of you. He'd have you by the throat."

"*If* he could get in," Gibson said. "There's only one entrance into that room and believe me, you need some pretty heavy ID to pass through."

Kimberly scanned the room jotting notes on her pad. As overwhelming as she found this incredibly sophisticated installation, she was equally impressed that half a dozen youngish men were standing around in shirt sleeves, some of them glancing at the continuing stream of computer read-outs, but mostly chatting and drinking coffee. They seemed completely relaxed and confident.

"I'm a little surprised," Kimberly said.

Gibson looked at her quizzically.

"Well, I understand that this is the control center, nerve center you called it. I'd have thought that someone a little more mature—

I mean, these guys look like they're working their way up from being assistant manager in a supermarket."

Gibson laughed. "Don't let their age fool you. Or the casual style. This is a young industry. Know where we recruit most of our people?"

"No," Kimberly said.

"From nuclear subs. After they've done a hitch or two. Where else would we find people who have experience in this sort of activity?"

"Glad you brought that up," Kimberly said, "I can use—"

"As for casual," Gibson went on, "one of the things these guys learn is to stay cool under stress. They wouldn't be acceptable on subs unless they've been tested for that. And that's exactly the kind of personnel we're looking for."

"Uh, wait a minute—I see an older guy," Richard said, pointing to a thickset man who lumbered out of an office and seated himself heavily in front of a desk. When he turned around to talk to one of the other men in the control room, Kimberly could see that his hard hat said: Ted Spindler, SENIOR REACTOR TECHNICIAN WORLD'S GREATEST FISHERMAN.

"He's the only one down there who looks old enough to know what he's doing," Richard remarked.

"Well, well, well," Kimberly chose to needle. "I thought you wouldn't trust anyone over thirty."

"That was before I reached thirty," Adams grinned back.

"Ted Spindler," Gibson said. "Good man. He

was with the company even before this plant was built. One of the few people who's made the transition from conventional generating technology to nuclear technology. Oh—uh, Adams!" Gibson's voice rose on a warning note as Richard lifted his camera to his shoulder.

"I thought you understood. No shooting in this area. There are obvious security reasons for that and some that aren't so obvious. At least not to you and me. But some of that stuff down there, as I understand it, might be of value to potential enemies. So if you don't mind —anybody want something to drink?" He gestured toward a Coke machine in an attempt to soften his injunction.

"Just one little shot, puleeze?" Richard played at being impish.

"Goddamnit, Richard—" Kimberly was obviously upset.

"Awright, awright. If you don't ask, you don't get, right?"

"But he already *told* you—"

"Coke, Kimberly?" Gibson said.

"No, thanks," Kimberly said, biting her lip. Richard was really beginning to get under her skin and she warned herself that she didn't have time for that. Personal concerns loused up professional judgment. It was something she had had to learn the hard way a while back and it was difficult for it to stay learned. Do you want to get ahead in this business, Kimberly asked herself, and responded, I *do* want to get ahead. Then shut up, she warned herself, and don't let that idiot bug you.

Hector was smiling and just reaching to

take a Coke from Gibson when a violent tremor hit the visitor's gallery and visibly shook the control room beneath them.

"Earthquake!" Richard shouted.

"What! What happened!" Kimberly was startled, frightened. She braced herself for another shock. But it did not come.

Gibson pressed against the glass and stared down at the control room. More technicians were now in the room and they were obviously excited. One of them could be seen yelling to an office nearby. The news team couldn't hear the voices below but they could sense the rising tension.

Appearing out of an office marked Shift Supervisor, Jack Godell stepped nimbly into the control room. A lean, wiry man in his late forties, with the quick, economical body movements of a dancer Godell brought with him an air of total authority.

"Ted!" his voice snapped out sharply.

"Turbine trip-out," Spindler replied over his shoulder, turning his head back immediately to keep his gaze on a bank of indicators above his desk.

Godell shrugged and the motion was immediately noted by all the other technicians in the room. One could almost see the excitement needle move down the scale a few indices. Warning lights were flashing and an annunciator was emitting a high-pitched warble. But Godell stood calmly in front of a table-top computer, holding the print-out sheet with one hand and an only slightly smoked cigar with the other.

Godell read from the computer print-out sheet in a sing-song tone, "Full load rejection."

Spindler replied on cue, "Reactor scram."

"Okay," Godell sighed, "looks like what we've got here is just a simple—"

Suddenly the room began to vibrate, slightly at first, but then more violently. A half-filled coffee cup waltzed to the edge of a counter and teetered there but Godell caught it. The other men in the control room froze at their positions. The shudder tapered down slowly, as the news team up in the visitor's gallery looked down on the scene, their faces ashen.

Richard Adams glanced at Gibson, saw that he was intensly focused on the scene below and surreptitiously switched his camera on, holding it at his hip on the far side of his body so that he wouldn't be detected. He flashed a glance at Kimberly but saw that she was also concentrating on the scene below. Nobody had noticed.

The vibration finally ceased. In the control room, Godell, frowning, swept his eyes over the banks of flashing lights. Suddenly, a loud, insistent alarm beeper rose above the ambient noise. Godell swung his gaze to a bank of annunciators.

"Radiation! Radiation in the containment!" The technician's voice was high with anxiety.

"Relax, Borden!" Godell rapped out a command. "Go down to instrumentation and get me core temperature at the rack. You, Holt—go to the rack and confirm Reactor SCRAM. I want positive confirmation again. Barney—come here! Watch the delta-P and shout those numbers out if they get over a hundred." Godell paused and shot a glance at Spindler. "What do you think?"

Spindler shrugged. "We better check out the steam loop."

"Makes sense," Godell grunted. He began moving quickly around the large room, Spindler at his side, checking various indicators, flashers, dials. Spindler jotted figures down from time to time on his clipboard. They were at home in this maze of electronic devices, as familiar with all these symbols as a woodsman with the forest. And they were completely oblivious to the tension and controlled excitement of the men around them, to say nothing of the reactions of the visitors in the gallery above. Total professionals, they were engrossed with the problem at hand.

"Will somebody please kill those goddamn alarm bells!" Godell bawled, adjusting his spectacles so that he could better read a dial. "I can't hear myself think."

Someone hit a switch and the worst of the hysterical noise fell away.

Moving quickly but deliberately in his rounds of the indicators above the consoles, Godell paused in front of a computer and read the tape.

"Event. Event. Event." He read. "Time start, 3:33:15. Reactor pressure limits exceeded. Turbine control valves 11-E5 and 11-E6 open. Turbine trip-out. Full load rejection. Reactor SCRAM. SCRAM. SCRAM."

Godell looked up from his reading of the electronic Gospel. He was like a priest pausing to lift his head up from his breviary. With the alarm silenced, the room was much quieter now but the men were edgy, waiting. Alarm lights continued to flash from red to green to amber and back to red again. From far below them there could be heard a distant rumble which he knew to be the venting of steam.

Keeping his voice low, Godell announced, "Looks like we have a turbine trip-out, fellas. Everybody within parameters?"

One by one the technicians confirmed that, in the area of their immediate responsibility, signals were within the acceptable range. Godell nodded and the tension in the room seemed to subside again.

Up in the visitor's gallery, the TV news team let out deep breaths and looked at each other. Richard edged a step further away from Gibson so that the PR man could not see that his camera was running. The phone rang and Gibson reached for it.

"Whatever was going on down there," Kimberly said, "it looks like it's done now. My God! do you suppose that's normal? I mean the whole building shaking. And when you think how huge this thing is and the power of those machines. . ."

She was interrupted by Gibson's voice on the telephone. He had dropped every trace of his genial host routine now and appeared much more serious. "Yeah, Jack. Bill Gibson up here in the visitor's gallery. That's right. TV news team. No, not filming. Of course not"

Kimberly glanced at Richard and was astonished to see that his camera was not only working, but that he was moving his body in such a way that the camera could pan slowly over the entire control room below. She looked at Gibson to see if he noticed and saw that he had not, then she sought Richard's eyes with her own. He argued with her silently, entreating her to be quiet.

"What's that?" Gibson went on.

"Uh, Richard," Kimberly said softly, moving a pace or two closer to the cameraman.

Gibson was still facing the wall, talking into the phone.

"Richard!" Kimberly protested, but wordlessly she moved closer, her clipboard shielding his camera.

Suddenly, a loud annunciator switched on in the control room below. They could hear the electronic yawp even through the double bullet-proof panels of glass in front of them.

Godell quickly put down the phone in the control room and turned to glance at a technician who was visibly upset. Then he moved next to Spindler who was gazing intently at a bank of dials.

"High-level warning," the technician called out, his voice rising. Neither Spindler nor Godell turned their heads.

Another technican called out, "Delta-P, one-zero-four!"

"That's a roger," Godell answered, keeping his eyes fixed on a set of indicators.

Up above this tumult, in the visitor's gallery, the news team watched with a mixture of fear and admiration as the control team went through their routines. It was almost like a ballet, Kimberly thought, people moving in almost ritualistic steps, bobbing, side-stepping, taking notes, adjusting switches, control handles, the entire team functioning as if they were not only superbly rehearsed, but closely directed.

They were startled by an amplified voice that issued from a P.A. system overhead. "All personnel proceed to designated safety areas. Code Six. All personnel proceed to designated safety areas. Code Six. This is not a drill. Repeat, this is not a drill."

Kimberly looked at Gibson.

"We stay right here," Gibson said tersely. "This is a safety area."

"But—"

"We stay right here."

"What's going on, Gibson?" Adams asked. "I mean, is this a routine or an emergency? What was all that shuddering?"

"I don't know," Gibson said. "They'll handle it down there. They're trained to handle it and they will. Meanwhile we stay right here."

Kimberly and Richard Adams exchanged glances. Richard's camera continued to roll.

In the control room, Godell had moved away from Spindler's console so that he now stood very nearly in the center of the room. His glance quickly took in all of the technicians and on some of their faces, there were signs of near panic.

"All right now," Godell said quietly but firmly, "everybody back off a notch. Relax. We've got high water in the core. I'm going to dump it. Meanwhile, somebody try to figure out where the goddamn water is coming from. You're paid to think under pressure, so start thinking and stop flapping." He moved together with Spindler to the water level indicator which clearly showed that the water level in the reactor core was above the area designated as normal.

"Wherever it's coming from, Ted, we'd better get the hell rid of it Open twenty-four and twenty-five *and* twenty-six," Godell called out.

Spindler's voice grated with concern. "You can't do that Jack, those—"

"I said do it," Godell repeated, his voice taking on a submarine skipper's rasp.

"But the book says you can't—"

"Screw the book, Ted," Godell said and then added, "Christ, we're almost up to the steam lines."

"Jack!" a technician called out, "it's got to be one of the valves, a feedwater leak. At least, that's all I can figure."

"Yeah, sure but which valve?" Godell asked.

"Not sure yet."

"Then shut the goddamn main."

"But Jack—"

"Mister," Godell lashed out, "would you rather go down into the hole and close the goddamn things by hand?"

Chastened, the technician reached for a pair of control handles. "Closing feedwater main!" he called out.

Goddell nodded and then turned his attention back to the bank of indicators over Spindler's head. Although he was tense, he was functioning rationally, coolly, efficiently. Unconsciously, many of the technicians, those not assigned to stations, had gravitated close to Godell, almost as if he were an island of calm in the middle of a tempest.

Out of the corner of his eye, Godell became aware of the growing encirclement. He'd experienced this sort of thing before at sea and was not startled by it, merely annoyed.

"All right, everybody! We can handle the goddamn feedwater without a goddamn kaffee klatsch!"

"Jack!" a technician called.

"I said cool it! Everybody!"

"Jack," the technician implored, "for God's sake—"

"What is it?"

"Your outflow! Look at it!" Godell shifted his gaze to another instrument beside the Core Level Indicator and saw that he was getting a contradictory reading. Godell frowned, looked back at the Core Level Indicator, still showing high water, then tapped the outflow indicator with his fingertip. The needle sank to the bottom of the chart.

"Jesus!" Spindler whispered.

"Feedwater!" Godell snapped. "Fast. Gimme feedwater. We're about to uncover the goddamn cooker."

Up in the visitor's gallery and throughout the entire plant, warning klaxons were beginning to sound. Gibson continued to lean on the desk overlooking the control room, his shoulders hunched, chewing a corner of his lip. Richard looked anxious but also smug. Kimberly had often seen this look on the faces of newsmen and it sometimes caused her to ask herself if this was a profession that she wanted to pursue.

Back in the control room, Godell's glance darted lizardlike from one monitor to the next. "Where we at now, Barney?" he called.

"One-thirteen," Barney answered.

"Christ," Spindler said, half under his breath, "that's less than nine inches, Jack."

Godell muttered something unintelligible and called out to Barney again. "Is it holding?"

"It's dropping, Jack."

"Good Christ," Godell said to Spindler, "we're losing it. It's the back pressure, Ted. Dump it, for God's sake."

"Jack, no—"

Godell reached brusquely across Spindler's body and grabbed a control handle. He hesitated for a fraction of a second and then slammed the handle down.

An immediate shudder emanated from deep within the bowels of the plant and communicated itself almost instantly throughout the entire installation.

A voice rang out. "One twelve!"

"Eight inches! Oh, my Christ!" Spindler groaned.

Godell ignored him. He was talking to the monitor, entreating it, coercing it. "Go, baby, go. Water. Agua. Cover it up, baby, cover up that mother-fucker. I mean, *now!*"

"Jack!" The voice was exultant. "It's holding!"

Godell didn't move at first. Then slowly, his

body straightened and he allowed his hand to slip off the control handle, his eyes fixed on the monitor above his head. The needle began to inch its way upward. And even though he kept his eye on the needle, he was aware that, in his peripheral vision, red warning lights were beginning to fade off the indicator panels throughout the room. As he regained an erect position, Godell allowed his hand to trail briefly across Spindler's shoulder. It wasn't much of an apology, nor much of an acknowledgment for Spindler's totally justifiable fear, but it would have to do.

As the annunciator beeps and alarm buzzers switched off, Jack called out to the technicians. "Okay, guys," he said tiredly, "read it to me. Reactor water level?"

"Stable," a voice called out.

"Stable," another voice confirmed.

"Core temp?" Godell raised his glasses and rubbed his eyes.

"Five-five-zero, Jack."

"Containment pressure?"

"Point-zero-five atmospheres."

"Stable shutdown?"

"Stable shutdown."

"Confirming stable shutdown."

"Event ends?"

"Three-thirty-six P."

"Event duration?"

"Two-point-four-five."

"Well, gents," Godell said, pushing himself wearily away from Spindler's console, "I guess that's it," he sighed.

TWO

It was dusk when they reached the TV studio and they were all out of the jeep almost before it had come to a stop. They raced up a flight of stairs and down a corridor, adrenalin pumping.

"Mort, save me!" Richard shouted, throwing open the film lab door. A tall, gangling, long-haired film technician, wearing a rubber apron, stood watch over large stainless-steel revolving drums.

"How y'all?"

"Mort, really," Richard entreated, "this is rush city."

"It's for me, Mort. We want to make the six—"

Mort cut Kimberly short. "So's all this other stuff. Priorities, baby, priorities."

"For me, Mort, please?" Kimberly coaxed.

"Will you go to a hot tub party with me tonight?"

"You're a doll, Mort. Richard, you stay right here and wait for it, will you? I'll be in the news room."

As she left, Mort turned to Adams. "What's

so special, she's comin' on like Linda Lovelace?"

"Dynamite!" Richard grinned contentedly. "Just cook the film, will you, dad? Like nuclear dynamite."

Upstairs, Kimberly burst into the newsroom at a fast trot. The room was crowded with reporters, newscasters, researchers and editors preparing for the six o'clock news.

Kimberly popped her head into an office. "There was an accident, Mac. Well, a near accident, anyway. And Richard got it all. I mean he got all the commotion in the control room. The nerve center."

Mac Harkness looked up from a teletype he was reading. "What in hell are you—"

"Ventana. The nuclear generating plant. Talk to you later." Kimberly slid out of the doorway and crossed to the wire service room. Long sheets of wire copy were hung on spikes, broken down into categories—international, national, local, politics, entertainment. Kimberly quickly riffled through to see if the wire services had begun to file anything on the Ventana plant yet, and found nothing. She still had an exclusive!

Passing the switchboard, she picked up a handful of telephone messages from the operator. "Anything heavy, Marge?"

"Nothing urgent," Marge said, "except your mother. How did a nice girl like you get a mother like that? Four times she called, and chewed me up one side and down the other because I wouldn't put out a missing persons bulletin on you."

"Dear ol' Mom," Kimberly said. "She's been called demanding. Wait—she's not calling from L.A., I hope."

"No, Sacramento. Call her, will you? Get her off me."

Kimberly grinned and made her way into her own office.

Cradling the telephone under her cheek as she examined the small sheaf of pink phone messages, she dialed the Sacramento number.

"Hi, Mom, your long lost—

"Oh. Well, I've been kinda b—

"That's right, too busy to get to a phone.

"Mother, would you mind telling me what's up? I've got a job to—

"A week from Thursday night! Which Thursday night?

"I did? I promised? All right, all right. I'll be there. Count on it, O.K.? Now I've got to go. How's dad? He is, eh? Good for him. No. Not yet, mother. As soon as they make me the anchorperson, you'll be the first to know. Right. Love you too. Ciao."

Kimberly let the phone slide to the cradle and heaved a sigh of exhaustion. For the moment, all the excitement had fizzed out of her bloodstream. She looked up as Mac poked his head through her doorway.

"What accident?" he asked.

"What?" Kimberly replied dully.

"Accident. You said—"

"Oh, right! We were in the visitor's gallery. Richard Adams, Hector Salas and I—we're doing Ventana as part of the Energy Today thing, O.K.? We're looking down on the control room, the nerve center, they call it. I mean it's where the whole damn thing is run. And suddenly, all hell broke loose. Rumbling, shaking, shuddering. And all these engineer dudes running around. And scared, Mac I mean they were really, really scared. White-faced and starting to sweat. I mean, this was no drill, in fact the announcement on the . . . Look, I haven't got time now. I've got to write it. And Richard's downstairs waiting to get his film out of the tank. So you'd better hold me a spot, a minute at the very least."

"Hey, Kimberly, cool it, will you? How come there's no mention of any accident on the wire copy?"

"Because we were *there* and they weren't. We lucked out, Mac."

Impressed, but still dubious, Mac said, "We still have time. I'd better call Jacovich."

But Kimberly was no longer listening. She wound a sheet into her typewriter and began typing as fast as she could.

Twenty minutes later they were all grouped around a table-top movie screen in the 16mm film editing room. The film was rough and jerky, some of it blocked by the edge of the window frame, sometimes going out of focus, but essentially, it was a thorough visual recording of all that they had seen that afternoon. Richard was providing a running commentary: "Look at that! Fantastic! God, did I get lucky. Now watch this pan."

Kimberly restricted herself to answering questions from Mac and Don Jacovich, the station's programming director. When the film ended, Kimberly was triumphant. "I told you it was incredible. Authentic drama. High drama, and none of it faked. Here's my copy, Don. It may be a little long, I haven't had time to cut it yet, but it's a dove-tailed eyewitness account. We were there. Scared speechless by those rumbles. And all those alarm noises. And the PA system: 'This is not a drill. Repeat. This is not a drill. Proceed to a safe area.' "

As she talked, Jacovich was scanning her copy and as his eyes moved downward, Kimberly began to get a sinking feeling.

A telephone rang and Jacovich reached for it. He paused, read another paragraph and then picked up the phone. "Hello, Jacovich. Who? Oh, right. I'll be down there in a minute. Tell 'em to hang on."

He downed the phone, glanced at Kimberly and said, "Interesting."

"Did you say—" Richard began, but Kimberly cut him off with a glance.

"Be a little more interesting," Jacovich said, "if we had some idea what all this meant. The implications, I mean. You've got a lot of stuff happening but no context. I don't know what it means I'm no nuclear engineer. And as you may recall, there aren't too many—"

"My idea," Kimberly interrupted, "was to let the story follow the action. And let the film speak for itself. My God, you saw the panic, the movements. There isn't any *acting* going on down there, Don. Those are—"

"Uh, tell me something: Do those people—I mean Ventana? Do they know we've got this film?"

"No, Richard filmed from the hip and they didn't see him. When it was all over, Gibson got us out of there fast. I really felt sorry for the man. What had started out as a routine PR tour ended up as a super-embarrassment. He was red and apologetic, but what could he say: sorry folks, we just had a near-nuclear disaster?"

"What exactly did he say?" Mac asked.

"Nothing. I mean that's what he said. It was nothing, folks. He said it was a routine turbine trip. Routine! Nothing out of the ordinary. And all the time he kept edging us out the door."

Hector made one of his rare and typically gentle unsolicited comments. "Well, you have to understand, Kimberly, he was responsible for our safety. Responsible for our being there. Imagine how he must have felt."

Kimberly flashed a quick synthetic smile at Hector, then turned back to Jacovich. "Listen, Don, we'd better get this film downstairs right away. Doesn't matter if its rough, hell, it's eyewitness stuff. We've got less than five minutes to air time and I'd like to smooth my words, just a little."

"No way, kid."

"What?"

"Don't 'what' me, Kimberly. No way I'm going to put this on the air at six o'clock until we know what the hell is going down."

"Goddamnit, Don. It's a scoop, can't you see that!"

"This is 1978 and not 1928. We're doing a TV news broadcast, not a remake of *The Front Page*. I'm talking about media responsibility. Do you read me? Now, Mac, you be sure and lock that film in the vault tonight and we'll get this thing checked out first thing tomorrow morning. I'll call Gibson and explain that we have the film. I'll see you people."

Without waiting for any additional discussion, Jacovich turned and left the film lab. They were silent in his wake.

Avoiding her eyes, Richard said, "Kimberly, you better get up to the studio, you're gonna be late."

"Yeah, right." She looked like she was about to cry. "I'm not doing myself any good down here."

"Yeah." Richard was unable to keep the disgust from his voice, "Give me a call."

"Later," said Kimberly in a muffled voice as she walked out. Richard leaned against a counter as Mac rewound the film. "I'm not surprised," he muttered. "Not surprised at all. Kinda what I expected, only I guess I allowed myself to hope. I allowed myself to think that maybe this outfit might act like a news outfit and not like another branch of the establishment. Another hunk of bureaucracy."

Mac was accustomed to Richard's fulminations "You really shot this stuff all from the hip? Without the PR guy knowing what was going on?"

"That's about the size of it, pardner," Richard said sardonically. "Reckon they call me the fastest camera in the West. But it looks like I've been shot down."

Upstairs, the news studio was swarming. Kimberly made her way to the rear of the set where a make-up man awaited her. She had hardly sat down before he began dabbing pancake on her face. Further down the floor, near the stage, a floor-director with a stopwatch around her neck supervised the positioning of three cameramen focused on the news desk. To the left of the floor-director, a technician checked the teleprompter, making certain that the copy rolled up synchronously with a script he had in his hand. At one side of the set, the weatherman was preparing his information board with the help of a prop man. The anchorman, Pete Martin, already made-up, smoked a last cigarette and bantered with the crew. The director called out a warning: "One minute, everybody."

Kimberly took her gaze away from the mirror and looked about the studio until she located Don Jacovich. He was talking to Bill Gibson. Could Jacovich have notified Gibson in time to get him over to the studio this fast? Not possible. Then it must have been Gibson's initiative.

Kimberly sighed. She had mixed regret and admiration for Bill Gibson's professionalism. He was, she concluded, just doing his job. No, correct that, she told herself. Not just. He was doing it damned well. But where did that leave her—and Richard? Up you-know-where, she told herself, and without a you-know-what.

She and Richard really didn't know what the hell was going on. Yes, it was possible that they might have gone on the air with material that suggested far more drama, crisis, danger —call it what you will—than really occurred.

And yes, that might be a lit-tle bit irresponsible.

On the other hand . . .

And on the other hand . . .

There were lots of other hands, Kimberly thought. Maybe they had actually seen the beginning of a crisis which was averted only at the last moment. Certainly that's what it looked like, and what the film looked like, as well. There was nothing like having a filmed record of all that they'd seen. Her report, subjective though it might have been, would have been strongly supported by the actuality of film.

Might have been, she consoled herself. Might also have been a splashy moment for Kimberly Wells. A chance to show that she was not just a doll-shaped news reader, but someone who knew what to do with a fast breaking news event when it landed in her lap.

A voice interrupted her musing. "Kimberly Wells. You've got thirty seconds. Kimberly Wells."

She was out of her chair and moving down toward the stage.

Harmon's Bar & Grille looked as if it had been decorated by the set-designer of "Gilligan's Island" after a three-week drunk. There were palm mats, bamboo rafters, blow fish, conch shells, glass float balls and netting over everything except the back bar and the ladies' bathroom. And even that was designated Wahine or Nooky Nooky or some other quasi-

Hawaiian gobbledygook. Hamm's beer signs with their everlasting sky blue waters seemed to clash with the plastic Polynesian atmosphere but nobody objected. It was a little bit of Bora Bora set down in the San Fernando Valley and the regulars liked the fact that it reminded them of their years in the service —Navy, mostly—and that the beer was always ice cold.

For all of its tacky, South Pacific trinkets, Harmon's had, over the years, drawn a group of regular patrons, mostly from the Ventana plant, an unofficial employee social club. As a consequence, it had the comfortable front room atmosphere of a neighborhood pub. In a far recess of the room, three or four guys were lounging around a pool table drinking beer and playing Eight-ball. And at another table, midway between the bar and the juke box and with only a short run to the gents, Jack Godell and Ted Spindler sat hunched over their booze. It was Jack's favorite table and, as he was a bachelor and stopped by Harmon's almost every night in the week, the management kept a little "Reserved" sign on it that had been stolen from a San Francisco hotel.

Both men were in shirt-sleeves. Both were into their second Seagram's and Seven and neither was talking very much. They'd had a trying, if not to say, perilous afternoon and it was very good to be in this combination womb, clubhouse and bomb shelter.

Godell took a reading on their glasses and turned to call to Harry The Mix—Harry had a certificate over the back bar attesting to his completion of a course in "Mixology," hence the name. "Fry us up another round, will ya, kid?"

"No, hey, listen, Jack—" Spindler protested.

"Come on. You earned yourself a little R & R."

"Ain't that the truth," Spindler sighed, thinking once again about the events of the afternoon. "I'd like to sit here and get smashed but Alma's having the kids over for dinner, and if I don't go by the store and pick up some chocolate ice cream, my littlest grandchild really chews me out. Sometimes I don't know whether to laugh at that little sprout or backhand her. What are ya gonna do?"

Godell wasn't exactly listening. He'd heard it all before and besides that, he was still too shaken by the afternoon's crisis.

"Twenty years of boredom," he'd said wryly, "twenty seconds of terror. That's what I'm going to call my autobiography. If I ever write my autobiography. If I live long enough."

"Yeah, well—" Spindler had heaved his bulk up out of his chair and was peeling off some bills. "Needless to say there'll be the usual witch hunt. They've always got to find someone, something to hang the blame on. How long do you reckon it'll be before the snoops are climbing all over us?"

"First thing tomorrow morning. Ordinarily, they'd wait a couple of days. Really tool up for it. But they haven't got time for that now. Not with those hearings due on the Point Conception lash-up. They'll want to get this bandaged up fast."

"Right," Spindler said. "Then I better make an early night of it. See you Jack. Come and see us."

Jack waved glumly, and resumed staring into his glass. He felt old and tired, and worst of all, he felt stretched. The anomaly at the plant that afternoon had tested him to the utmost, had called on all his stores of experience, intuition, native intelligence. All of it. He knew, when the crisis was over, that he'd nothing left in reserve. And that scared him. What would he be able to come up with the next time that occurred? Well, he consoled himself, he was still here, they all were, and somehow they had muddled through. But only by the very thinnest skin of their teeth.

Godell had been the engineering officer on a nuclear submarine, with full responsibility for plant operation. And he'd been with the Ventana plant since the very beginning. He did not, or had not until today, doubted his competency. What disturbed him about the events of the past afternoon was that he'd *thought* he had the solution to the problem, only to have to turn around and reverse himself completely at the last minute. And it was, he knew, the last minute. One more . . . he shuddered.

His musing was interrupted by the arrival of Harry The Mix with his fresh drink. "Hey, you'll stay for another, won't you," Harry said. "Next one's on the house."

"No thanks, Harry," Godell looked up. "This ought to top off my tank. Hey—that the news on TV? Turn it up a little, will you?"

Jack picked up his drink and walked over to

the bar so that he could get a direct sight line to the color TV. He was just in time to see Pete Martin flashing his dentures and announcing, "And now here's Kimberly Wells with California Closeup."

Jack stared moodily as Kimberly Wells smiled into the camera and began to read, "The hottest young designer in Hollywood these days is not designing for women but for men."

Jack swung around on his stool and addressed Harry. "Hey, Mix, you been watching the news?"

"Uh, yeah, a little, you know."

"They have anything on the Ventana plant so far?" Jack asked. "Anything about us shutting down?"

"Oh? You guys shut down?" Harry asked. "No, I didn't catch anything like that. I been behind the bar except when I brought you your drink and I think that was on a commercial."

Godell grunted with relief.

"What's this about a shutdown? Couldn't pay your electric bill?"

Jack grinned, although it might have been an expression of pain. "That's very witty, Harry. I hope you'll keep up the good work. Your humor is getting better all the time. Soon you'll be able to bring it up to lousy."

His eyes swung back to Kimberly who was fondling fabrics. He sighed deeply, took another long pull of his drink and suddenly realized that he needed fresh air fast.

Staggering off his stool, he made a signal to Harry to put the drink on his tab and lurched out into the gathering darkness. It wasn't much cooler outdoors than it was in the bar but the sudden drop-off in jukebox music was a restorative. He checked his reflexes, took a few deep breaths and decided he could just about, if he was slow and careful, drive himself safely home. Home wasn't very far away, within walking distance, in fact, and he'd made the distance many times on foot. Home, he thought to himself. Home. A place with an air conditioner, a TV set and a fridge full of TV dinners. It occurred to him for just a micro-second that his life was almost unbearably drab. And no sooner did that flash occur than he reacted with the speed of a computer, to shut down the signal. Get in the car, boy, he told himself, point it carefully and steady as you go.

If someone had told Jack that he was an automaton, that he was a technician who was fast becoming de-humanized by his absorption with techology, that he was a lonely, haunted man and in fact, a tragic figure, a by-product of the nuclear age—if someone had said any or all of these things, Jack would have snorted contemptuously.

But no one ever told him anyway.

While Jack Godell was pondering his cache of TV dinners, wondering whether he was going to gag on Swiss Steak or Baked Virginia Ham Surprise, or whether he ought to forget the whole thing and just finish the evening on bourbon and salted peanuts, Herman De Young was walking softly down the cushioned corridors of Cal. Gas & Electric. The building, old-fashioned among the glittering new high-rise structures in downtown L.A., was something of a landmark, both inside and out. The exterior reflected the baroque and exuberant architectural style of the mid-twenties. The interiors at the executive level were even more ornate with thick oriental rugs, hand-rubbed walnut paneling, manneristic portraits of top executives in gilt frames, crystal chandeliers and over all, the tangy, intoxicating scent of money and power. Every time De Young left his Spartan premises at Ventana to come down to headquarters, he felt that he was making a journey to Mt. Olympus.

He paused before a door marked EVAN MacCORMACK, CHAIRMAN, C.G.&E. The door was open and there were lights inside. De Young paused and bethought himself. MacCormack, he knew, was a notorious womanizer who hired his secretaries the way old-time movie producers used to hire starlets. He might be in the midst of breaking in a new girl. On the other hand, De Young told himself, MacCormack didn't get where he was by being so stupid as to permit himself to be caught *in flagrante* by a cleaning woman or a late working executive. He padded silently into the office, passed through the ante-room and into the vast walnut-paneled cave where the chairman dwelled.

Knocking discreetly on the half-open door, De Young went into the inner office where he saw MacCormack and a man he recognized as Gordon Hatcher, financial vice president, both watching a news broadcast on TV. MacCormack, glanced up at De Young and waved him in.

"Come on in, Herman. Hatcher was just saying—go on, Gordon. You know Herman De Young, of course."

"Sure. 'Evening, Herman. I was saying that if the permit on our Point Conception installation is delayed for any appreciable length of time, our cash flow dries up. I got a call from Goldman Ferman this morning and the gossip on Wall Street is that our bond rating may be up for review. Now, as you both know, that process can drag on for months, and in the meanwhile, we won't be able to borrow a nickel." Hatcher paused and took a deep breath.

"What's more," he continued, "there's a rumor going around that the Public Utilities Commission is going to deny our latest rate increase. Now you know and I know that they *always* deny the request for a rate increase and that sooner or later, they grant it. Politics as usual. But still, it ties us up financially. And finally, one more thing: we're carrying heavy debts on the power grid to every other utility west of the Rockies. So in a very real sense, we're already heavily mortgaged. I'm not talking disaster, mind you. But I don't think we can be complacent either."

"About our power indebtedness," MacCormack said, "would you spell that out roughly?"

"How about exactly?" Hatcher answered, opening a file of papers. "We'll be losing four hundred ninety-two thousand dollars a day. That's net."

MacCormack tugged at his chin. "And now the bad news."

They all laughed dutifully.

De Young cleared his throat. "Speaking for my operation, our first assessment, and I'd say it's a fairly thorough one, that is, we don't expect any major surprises—we've no damage. Oh, sure, there's clean-up to do and some minor repairing but no substantial capital outlay is anticipated. Of course, there will also have to be an accident hearing."

"Formal, you mean?" Hatcher asked. "The usual rigamarole going on for anywhere from a week to—"

"I should think this would be fairly brief. The Nuclear Regulating Commission is sending out a team of investigators first thing in the morning. And we'll be testifying starting tomorrow."

"Can you be back on-line by the end of the week?" MacCormack asked.

De Young paused. He understood the folkways of the American corporate system well enough to know that top executives sought and elicited up-beat answers. What they didn't want was gloom or doubt of doubtful prognoses. On the other hand, they didn't want to be fooled by rosy forecasts which turned out to be catastrophic. A pause gave De Young the opportunity to re-group. "I should say," he kept his voice firm but deferential, "that it is not only possible but that there is a high degree of probability we'll be on-line by the end of the week. Barring, of course, the unforeseen. And needless to say, if anything turns up, any road block that we haven't anticipated, I'll notify this office at once and give you an updated timetable."

"Sounds as if you're on top of it, Herman," MacCormack said easily, "and I want you to keep at it. The way you're going. Keep that investigation on point. Overlook nothing, make sure that you're using your time to good advantage. We don't want a recurrence of the defect six months from now. On the other hand—" He paused ominously. "Time is of the essence. You understand that. So let's get this thing done as quickly as possible."

"Yes, sir," De Young said.

"And I hope," MacCormack said, in a tone that was both pious and admonitory as well, "we've had the last of our surprises out there at Ventana. Had enough to last us for the year."

"I agree," De Young said. There was nothing else he could say. It occurred to him that it was a terrible thing to be forty-seven years old and standing on the chairman's carpet quaking inwardly like a small child and feeling a lump at the pit of his stomach.

Having flicked the corporate lash ever so slightly, MacCormack was now ready to be benign. At his bar he poured tumblers full of his second-best twenty-year-old bourbon, and was handing out the glasses when the phone rang.

He answered and listened for a moment, murmuring to De Young, "It's Bill Gibson. Yes, Bill, go on. No, I didn't see anything on TV. That's good work, you're to be complimented. Herman De Young is here in my office. I understand the Nuclear Regulatory Commission has already been notified, so that means the thing will be public tomorrow morning. We'd better have our press releases ready . . . Oh, you did? Very good. Needless to say, we'll have to announce shutdown tomorrow morning. Perhaps you and I had better have breakfast together . . . Film? What film? What are you—wait a minute, I want the others to hear this."

MacCormack pressed a switch and Bill Gibson's voice now came out of a small amplifier on his desk, audible to the other men in the room.

"They were in the visitors gallery above the control room," Gibson was saying. "And of course, I was with them and I had given this cameraman strict orders not to film down there. Well, it appears he did it anyway, without my realizing it. You've got to understand, it was a pretty tense moment and I was focused on all that hubbub down in the control room. Perhaps if I hadn't been, I might have been able to stop him."

"That's all right, Bill," MacCormack broke in. "It was a natural human reaction. So the crafty little son of a bitch sneaked some footage while our backs were turned, so to speak. That really burns me up. I think our legal people may find this actionable, not only a cause of action against the cameraman, but against the TV station as well. Hell, he's their agent, they have to accept responsibility for his behavior. In any case, you plan on meeting me here at eight-thirty tomorrow morning, Bill. We'll have some breakfast and take it from there."

"Will do," Gibson said. "Good night, all."

MacCormack put the phone back on its cradle and turned to the others. The expression on his face was now anything but benign. He looked, De Young thought, mean and angry and as tough as nails.

"I don't know," MacCormack said, "just what we can do about this film business. I won't know that until I know just what those people have got on film and how it might prejudice our interests. But if those Hollywood TV bastards think they can monkey around with a company like this, they've got another think coming. Herman, you make damn sure that bunch doesn't get near the plant without getting direct authorization from me."

"Yes, sir. I assure you—"

"You don't have to assure me of a damn thing. I'm not blaming you and I'm not blaming Bill Gibson. Not yet. But this company's got its fanny on the line and starting right now we're all going on picket duty. That's all I have to say. Let's call it a night."

THREE

Kimberly Wells was moving briskly down a corridor of the TV studio, carrying her morning coffee and a pineapple Danish, when she heard a familiar hullabaloo. What was familiar about it, she realized, as she stopped short to listen and snatch a bite out of her Danish, was Richard's voice raised in anger. As usual, there wasn't any other voice because it was impossible to get in a word or even a shriek edgewise, until Richard's rage had run its course.

"Goddamnit, you've got to put it on the air," she heard. "You've got no choice. It's a goddamn bona fide news event. If a nuclear accident isn't a news event, what the hell is? This was a nuclear accident. And I photographed it, and you're sitting on top of a priceless can of film and giving me bullshit answers."

"Wrong," Kimberly heard. "I haven't given you any answers so far and I won't until you stop hollering in here like a goddamn fourth-grader." By this time, Kimberly was close enough to the door so that she could recognize the voice. Jacovich. She opened the door to the conference room and peered in. Richard was striding around the room like a man beset by hornets. Jacovich sat calmly in a chair, watching him. Mac stood by, frowning but concerned.

"To begin with," Jacovich said, glancing up and motioning Kimberly to enter, "I'm not sure and *you're* not sure that accident is the right word. Maybe that's not what you saw."

"Sorry I'm late," Kimberly said. "Car trouble. Anybody want a bite?"

Jacovich smiled wanly, declining. Richard glowered and threw his hands up in a gesture of despair.

"Oh it's the right word, all right," Richard said. "I know what we saw and what *you* saw too, Kimberly. Christ, you were there. You felt it, saw it. How does it feel to be working for a TV station with a yellow streak down its back? I mean a big yellow streak. About that wide."

Kimberly felt impelled to search her memory. Was there any possibility that what they had experienced was merely routine? What about those tremors? Shudders, really. Very much like an earthquake. And what about those anxious men, sweating, white-faced, moving around that control room with panic on their faces and shouting at times so loudly that you could hear their voices through the bullet-proof glass? And finally, what about that P.A system ordering all personnel to safe areas? "This is *not* a drill. Repeat, this is not a drill." No, she thought, there was no doubt in her mind about what she'd seen.

"It appears to me," she said evenly to Jacovich, "that you've already made your decision. Regardless of whatever Richard and I have to say. Is that right?"

"Now don't you start in on me too, Kimberly."

"Start in! I've barely opened my mouth. Or aren't I supposed to do that, either."

"Let me read you something," Jacovich said, taking up a paper and putting on his glasses. "Um mm mm—here it is: Nuclear plants are considered 'security installations, and as such, fall under the protection of Title 18 of the U.S. Criminal Code. Unauthorized photography is a *felony.*' "

Jacovich looked up at them to re-enforce his point. "So in the strictest technical sense, you people have committed a felony and we, all of the executives responsible at this station, could be considered accessories to a felony just for having the film on the premises, to say nothing of putting it on the air. Are you aware of the legal ramifications?"

"You can ram your ramifications, Jacovich, ram 'em and jam 'em. It's just more of the same old establishment bullshit. 'We want all the power and we'll take none of the risks.' Makes me so fuckin' mad I could—ouch, goddamnit, don't kick me, Kimberly."

"All right, I'm sorry, Richard, but, for God's sake, calm down. I've as much right to be sore as you."

"Bullshit," Richard snapped. "You're buying their bullshit. They want you to be calm. Here, look at this!" He slapped a creased, well-thumbed press release in front of her, but before she could see what it was, he read it for her.

"'Due to an unanticipated transient, it has been decided to close down the Ventana plant' . . . unanticipated transient, for Christsake. Did you ever hear such malarkey in your life! We're talking about an accident or a near-accident. It could have killed us. Could have killed half the goddamn county for all I know and they're talking about an unanticipated transient. That sounds like some bum who came by unexpectedly, looking for a cup of coffee. This is pure, one hundred per cent PR bullshit. And they're buying it."

"Aren't you maybe over-reacting, Richard? Killed us, killed half the country. I mean, in fairness, how do we *know*? *What* do we know? We know what we saw but we don't know what it signifies."

"Oh, shit, I give up," Richard said. "I mean when you begin to doubt your own perceptions, baby, you're washed up as a newsman. You're just—"

"According to C.G.&E." Jacovich said sharply, "you people were in no real danger at any time. We have their assurances on that."

"Well, of course they'd say that!" Richard started to bellow again but Kimberly managed to cut him off.

"Knock it off, Richard," she said shrilly. She turned to Jacovich. "I understand what you're saying, Don, and you can see that I'm trying to be fair-minded about this thing. But Richard has a point too. It's hard to think there was no danger when you were there. When you went through what we did. We saw the panic on those faces. We felt that huge establishment shaking exactly as if there was an earthquake. And finally, we heard that P.A. system ordering people to safe areas. And repeating: 'This is not a drill.' Now, when you put that all together with the film, it's hard not to believe that something extraordinary wasn't going on. I think we need another opinion. I think this film ought to be shown to an expert."

"No way," Jacovitch said. "That film stays in the vault. I'm not going to expose you and this station to felony charges."

"What you're gonna do," Richard said, hugely disgusted, "is sweep it under the rug. A matter of intense public interest, to say nothing of public safety. And you, the responsible TV executive is going to say, 'fuck the public, I'm looking after my own ass. I'm covering it up.' "

"You know, you're really starting to get me angry, Richard," Jacovich said. "I'm about to run out of patience with you. This is *not* a cover-up!"

"That's what tricky Dicky said. Right on the air. Right while he was covering things up. 'Let me make this perfectly clear—' "

"I said," Jacovich continued, "this is not a cover-up. There is no conspiracy between this station and C.G.&E. The plant had no obligation to contact the press on an internal matter. They did what they are required by law to do. They shut down the plant and they contacted the Nuclear Regulatory Commission. And an investigation has already begun."

"Who's doing the investigating?" Kimberly wanted to know.

"The NRC. We've asked for and we are entitled to a full report. The NRC is working in the public interest. At the time we get that report we'll decide what to do about this film."

"And it'll be dead. Dead as Kelsey's nuts. I can't believe this," Richard said. "Kimberly, are you just going to *sit* there? I mean, this is classic. One goddamn piece of the establishment looking after another piece of the establishment, covering up each other's asses. You don't think the NRC is going to come down on these guys, do you? Oh, they might make it look good. But the NRC boys and the private sector boys are like asshole buddies. The private sector takes these guys out to dinner and buys them chippies and flies them down to Bermuda. And then it hires them, for Christsake. You don't think this is going to be on the level, do you?"

"You leave Kimberly out of this," Jacovich said sternly. "It's not her business. And it isn't yours, either. This is a matter for the people who have to make policy. Both of you need to understand that this is a sensitive matter. And if you understand nothing else, you'd better realize that you've already committed a felony as defined by law and that you risk being sued I'll be damned if I'm going to see this station sued. Not if I can help it."

"Hey, Jacovich," Richard's voice suddenly went soft, ingratiating. "Tell me the truth. Where's the pressure coming from? Who's behind the squeeze?"

"There is no pressure, no squeeze. I'm doing what any sensible person would do in my position, with the facts that I've got before me."

"Oh, don't kid an old hand, Don," Richard went on. "I've been through this scene too many times. There's always a pressure point somewhere. I'm just asking who, that's all."

"There is no pressure," Jacovich repeated woodenly, "unless I count the pressure from you. And I consider you talented but an alarmist. In fact, I consider you hysterical."

"Well, it's always good to lay our cards on the table, Donny-boy," Richard said, "and I consider you a chicken-shit asshole!"

"Richard!" Kimberly shouted. But he was already out the door.

She turned to glance at Jacovich who was staring blankly into the middle distance like a man who has just barely missed being destroyed by a grenade burst. She could sympathize with him, to be sure, but there was another part of her that wanted to add the childish words: and that goes double—for me! She merely shrugged and went down the corridor until she found Richard straightening up over the water fountain.

"Boy," she said, trying to smile but still shaken by the ruckus inside, "you sure have a bad attitude, man."

"Bad attitude!" He laughed, then turned serious again. "They got to you, didn't they, Kimberly? Well, I'm not surprised. I've seen it happen before. People who fought beside me in the ranks, I mean really *fought*, and I've seen them bought off with this same kind of mealy-mouthed responsibility bullshit. We all want to be grown up. And that's how they get to you. They make you feel as if you're a child because you're shouting mad, as if there were something wrong about a grown-up screaming his head off at injustice. I tell you, that's not childish, that's right. That's sane. It's insane *not* to scream your head off. But they work that ploy. And they sucked you in."

"Oh, Christ," Kimberly groaned. "I am so bored with this routine of yours. This revolutionary veteran bit. If only you understood the techniques of the enemy, my children, you would see them for the beasts they really are.

"It's the same old crap you've been dishing out for years, Richard. Listen, I'm not ashamed to have a good job. Of making good money. I'm hoping not only to keep my job, but to go on to a better job and get even more money. So if that's what you mean about getting sucked in, you're damn right. I'm sucked in. And another thing, now that I think of it, you're the one who called me and said you were getting a little tired of the free-lance life and could you come inside out of the cold for a while, and could I throw you a bone. Is that right, or isn't it?"

Richard refused to answer. He merely shook his head as a gesture of futility and started striding down the corridor.

She ran a few steps after him. "Hey, we still have a lot of work to do on my features. The first one's got to be edited in the next few days, and—"

Richard kept on walking. He gave no sign that he'd heard.

Kimberly turned around, crestfallen, just in time to see Mac and Don Jacovich leaving the conference room. She hurried a few steps, reaching Mac just as Jacovich rounded a corner.

"I'd like to talk to Jacovich" she said, as Mac took her arm.

"Uh, better leave it, Kimberly," Mac said. "He's pretty scraped up right now. Leave it until tonight, until everybody's cooled down a little. By the way, they called from upstairs. The mini-cam van is waiting for you. You're doing a live spot at noon today, aren't you?"

"Yeah," Kimberly said, trying to keep her voice neutral and barely succeeding. "I'm going out to the zoo today, Mac. A lion is having a birthday party."

She turned and made her way downstairs to meet the mini-cam van, wondering if Richard's outburst would reflect on her, if she'd ever get a chance to do another serious story again.

Elsewhere in the building, in the basement, Richard made his way past the film lab, waved to his friend Mort, and pushed through a door into another corridor. This was a much quieter, dimmer place, with very little sign of human activity. And, at the far end of the corridor was a small sign that said, FILM VAULT.

By two o'clock in the afternoon, the principals of the accident investigation group were assembled in the main conference room at the Ventana plant. Officials of the Nuclear Regulatory Commission had arrived early and had spent the morning hours touring the plant, inspecting its facilities and making notes on what they had seen. It was time now to hear the verbal testimony of the Ventana executives and technicians and that procedure began immediately after lunch. A court reporter, equipped with a steno-type machine, recorded every word uttered in the session. It would form the record of this inquiry and provide future technicians with a verbal history of what had occurred.

Herman De Young sat at the head of the long table, flanked by plant engineers and lawyers. At the opposite end of the table sat Morton Robertson, a handsome and dapper nuclear engineer who headed up the inquiry team from NRC. He was accompanied by his aide, Kenneth Lever, an inscrutable young man who was reputed to have the speed and retention capability of a giant computer. Half a dozen other experts, some from Ventana, some from NRC, were grouped around the table.

It was Jack Godell's turn to speak, and he handled himself coolly, reasonably, referring now and again to mock-ups of the nuclear reactor which sat on a long table at one side of the room.

"Our analysis is," Godell was saying, "that a faulty relay in the generator circuit tripped the generator breakers open. The resulting transient in water level and pressure caused the turbine to trip and consequently caused safety relief valve number eight to open automatically. This created a sudden shutdown of the reactor. In other words, a SCRAM situation."

Robertson took advantage of a natural pause. "For the record, then, it was safety valve number eight. That, you say, is the valve that stuck open, thereupon releasing radiation into the containment. Am I tracking you?"

"Yes, sir, you are." Godell permitted himself a faint acknowledging smile. "That was the cause of radiation on levels six and eight going off-scale."

Robertson adjusted his glasses so that he could scan the event computer print-out sheet which he held in his hand "So except for the course of the second shock wave—"

"More like a shudder, sir. A heavy vibration. I realize we're into a slightly subjective area here, but—"

Robertson gestured: no matter. "Except for the 'shudder' you are clear in your mind. Up to this point."

"That's correct," Godell said. He was about to add a "sir," but bit it off at the last moment. This wasn't a Naval court of enquiry, after all.

Robertson continued to read the print-out sheet. "Now the reactor water level begins to drop—"

"Yes," Jack broke in, "but that's because we thought the water level was high. And we traced that to the fact that the pen in the Water Level Recorder stuck." He gestured.

"I see," Robertson said evenly. "So you began cutting off the feedwater flow and releasing steam in the belief that the water was too high. Is that correct?"

"Yes, sir, it is," Godell said. He was beginning to feel a touch uncomfortable and was irritated at his own reaction. After all, he had prepared himself mentally for these very questions and had analyzed his own actions as meticulously as he was able. Why the discomfort then? He didn't know.

"But in fact," Robertson's tone now became crisp, "the water level was becoming dangerously low. Is that correct?"

"Yes, sir."

"Uh, if I may . . ." Kenneth Lever, Robertson's young aide, touched his superior on the arm. He received a nod and proceeded with his question. "Why," he asked tonelessly, "didn't your operator query his other indicators?"

"I—" Godell paused and then spread his hands. "I don't know. But—" He paused again. "I don't think Ted Spindler should shoulder all the responsibility for this. It was a tense situation, things were happening fast. I was standing right beside Spindler and I didn't look at the other indicators either. Our major concern was with water level at that moment."

There was a silence in the conference room, unbroken except for the muffled sounds of the steno-type machine. Soon that came to a stop as well.

Robertson cleared his throat. "I think that will do for the moment, Mr. Godell. We'll excuse you for the time being and I think we'd like to hear from Mr. Spindler."

Godell nodded and, without looking at his boss, Herman De Young, made his way out of the conference room. Spindler was sitting outside with one of the younger control room technicians. They both quickened when Godell emerged.

"How'd it go in there?" Spindler asked.

Godell managed a weak grin. He gestured with his hands, half-good, half-bad. "O.K., I guess."

"What'd you tell them?"

Godell shrugged and grimaced. "You know the rules, Ted. They asked us not to discuss our testimony."

Spindler nodded and stared at the floor. The conference room door was opened and an aide called out, "Ted Spindler? Can you come in now, please?"

As Spindler stood up, Godell raised his hand in a thumbs-up gesture and went down the corridor in search of the can.

That night Kimberly stood on a terrace alongside a swimming pool, looking down on what she concluded was damn near the rest of L.A. The house, belonging to Don Jacovich, was set atop the highest of the many hills flanking the Los Angeles basin, and the whole gaudy, light-spangled megalopolis lay before her. This was the promise, she realized, the dream. The house on the hill, the commanding view, the swimming pool and the white-coated waiters in the background moving efficiently and with highly paid cordiality through tufts of beautiful people. Kimberly, herself, looked beautiful in something soft and white, her long red hair piled nonchalantly on her head, tendrils whispering around her elegant white neck. The new hairstyle was a real conversation piece, a fact that both delighted and disturbed Kimberly.

She had chatted with half a dozen people, three of whom had made routine passes, and the evening was still young. She hadn't yet found anyone terribly attractive but people usually drifted in and out of this kind of party and if she felt adventurous later on, she might just let herself get taken home. Feeling confident and aware that she'd reached that crucial metabolic state where more gin would make her woozy, she allowed herself to be guided to the elegant buffet.

Moments later, perched at an occasional table with a plateful of food, she became aware of a presence looming three points to starboard. She looked up and saw Don Jacovich holding a plate.

"May I?" he asked.

"Oh, Mr. Jacovich, certainly. It's a wonderful party."

He grunted, sitting down beside her so that their knees touched. "How can you keep your weight down when the company expects you to entertain on the grand scale? So tell me, what's with you? You shoot any more stuff on that energy special you're doing?"

"No." Kimberly decided to avoid every trace of irony. This was a party, after all, and it was bad manners to bring the office, the grubby politics of office life, up to this social oasis. "We're done shooting, except for an opening and a closing. But we'll get that done in the next couple of days. I think you're going to be pleased. Richard—I know, he's difficult—but he's by far the best cameraman I've ever worked with."

"I didn't know you'd worked with so many," Jacovich said, with no trace of bitchiness.

"Actually, I have, Don. Quite a few."

A butler refilled their wine glasses and removed Kimberly's plate.

"Where'd you find him? Whatsisname, Adams? I thought he was under contract to us. Until this afternoon when I called down to fire him. That's right, fire him. I don't like being called a chicken-shit asshole. In fact, I hate it. So that's personal. And in addition, I don't think it's good for the company to have people on staff who feel they can abuse executives in this way. It makes for lousy discipline and sloppy work."

Kimberly composed her reply carefully, keeping her voice modulated. "Well, there was no one in the camera pool when the features were assigned to me. So I had to scramble around for crew. Richard is someone I've known ever since my commercial days. He's as good as they come. He's won just about every top award—"

"I believe the awards," Jacovich said acidly. "The hot-head award, the foul-mouth award, the can-of-worms award. Bill Gibson, the PR guy over at Ventana, told me that Adams was making antinuclear statements and jokes all the time you people were shooting at the plant. That's bad manners, Kimberly. Is it true?"

"Yes, unfortunately, it is."

Jacovich sighed. He looked at her now without bitterness and his tone softened. "I hate to repeat myself, kid, but when you first came to work here, I did give you my balanced reporting speech, did I not? If not, I'll do it now."

"I remember it very well."

"Good," Jacovich said. "I'll recap it anyway. A reporter must learn to keep his—her opinion out of a story. I hope these features that you two are doing are not *visually* biased, if you know what I mean. A cameraman can put a lot of English on the ball. Not only by what he shoots, but how he lights it, what the sequence of shots is, the rhythm, all of those things. And what we're after is coverage in the first instance, not controversy. Not that we're trying to duck controversy, but our first responsibility . . ."

"What are you planning to do with that film?" Kimberly asked.

Jacovich took advantage of her question to spear food and shovel it furiously into his mouth. He looked, Kimberly thought, like some wide-mouthed fish working through a school of minnows.

"It's up to the legal people right now. They're sweating it. So don't you worry your pretty head about that end of it, we'll protect you if it comes to that."

A maid interrupted. "Coffee, ma'am?" she asked.

Kimberly nodded, "Yes, please."

Jacovich continued, his tone becoming unmistakably patronizing. "You just keep doing a good job. And you are, you know. A hell of a job. Research confirms that our ratings have gone up—just because of you. The truth, I kid you not."

Kimberly smiled appreciatively. "That's good, but I'd really like to work in harder news. I'd like to do some real reporting and not just—you know—fluff."

"You call your energy series fluff?"

"No, of course not. But you know what I mean, Don. I'm talking about fast breaking hard news, not just features. The energy series is service copy, not exactly news copy. I'm getting to be a big girl now and I'd like to join the A-team."

"I can understand that," Jacovich said, nodding equably, and reaching in his breast pocket for what Kimberly recognized as an atrociously expensive cigar.

He continued between puffs. "You see how these specials work out. I personally feel that you're better doing the softer stuff—no offense now. But let's face reality. You're the pretty one, Kimberly, the frosting on our cake. We may not like it but we're forced to give the public this kind of a mix."

"Are you sure? Has anyone ever gone out and asked the public?"

"Damn right we have. The ratings tell no lies, kid. Like it says in *Chorus Line*, tits and ass, tits and ass. You say you're a big girl now? O.K., face up to reality. You didn't get hired here just because of your investigative abilities. Oh, we didn't want a dummy, that's true. But we didn't want a dog either. So don't try to force yourself out of character. If it happens, it happens. But right now, I like you doing exactly what you're doing."

If Kimberly felt disappointment, and she did, massive disappointment, she did not permit herself to show it. She stared at him dispassionately for a moment, then smiled, took his cigar from his fingers and gave it a long puff. He grinned, relieved. She *was* cute, by God.

A couple came by, a young actress and a middle-aged director. Jacovich introduced them to Kimberly and took advantage of a lull to make his exit. She did not find herself close enough to speak to him for the rest of the evening. And on the whole, she concluded, that was probably a good thing.

Having collected her wrap and her purse, she was threading her way through the late-stayers near the pool, making her goodbyes, when Pete Martin clamped her arm. From the pressure alone, she knew that he was drunk.

He drew her close, breathing gin blasts into her hair. "Mac Churchill just told me," he panted, "that your cameraman, whatsisname, called Jacovich a chicken-shit asshole. And I just want to say: bully for him! Terrific. What's Jacovich been laying on you? I saw you two at dinner. He was defining your role at the station, right? That's his number one trip, role defining. Fuck 'em, kid. Don't pay any attention to him. I've got something to say about defining and you'd better believe it. I've got 'em by the short hairs on a five-year play or pay contract. So I can run some pretty heavy interference when I want to. You dig where I'm coming from?"

"Hey, that's real nice of you, Pete. I mean, really," Kimberly said idiotically, wondering how she was going to get away from his sodden embrace.

"Tell you what," Pete went on expansively, "how about you and me we get together for some role defining, okay? Hey, you wanna play cars?" He put both hands on her breasts and squeezed. "Honk, honk!"

Instinctively, Kimberly shoved him, a bit harder than she'd realized. Pete Martin, staggered backward into the swimming pool, the deep end.

It was to cheers and laughter that Kimberly made her exit.

Half an hour later she stood in the kitchen of her house in Laurel Canyon. She'd kicked off her shoes and put a zip-up sweat shirt over her dress. The house was cold and damp. Staring vacantly down at an ugly desert tortoise which she'd found in the Mojave Desert, she impulsively plucked him up and began to feed him alfalfa sprouts. What am I doing here, Kimberly asked herself, standing around in bare feet at one o'clock in the morning, feeding a dumb turtle I don't really want and which is beginning to stink and which may die in a week or two?

Putting down the tortoise, she crossed her arms to bring a bit more warmth to her body and looked around the house. There was almost no furniture in the place except for an expensive brass bedstead. Her clothes, books, other things were still in the same cardboard cartons they were delivered in. It looked, she thought, like a way station, not a home. More like a bus terminal. For transients, she told herself. For people on the move? Ho, ho, ho!

She moved to the telephone recording device to check the residue of messages accumulated during her absence. The machine began to play and she made herself a liverwurst sandwich from a refrigerator that looked enormous for just a quarter pound of butter, half a loaf of bread, a quarter bottle of fermenting wine and the stub of browning liverwurst.

"Hello, darling . . ." She recognized the voice, of course. Mother. "I hate talking into these things. Will you call me when you can?"

"Hi, Kim—it's Karen, I just called to chat. Nothing special. Later, okay?"

"Kimberly," a self-assured masculine voice boomed, "it's old uncle Buck Brewer. Surprised? I'm here from the Big Apple, love to see you. Call me at the Hillcrest, 233-3330, room 567. Call before eight. Caught you on the tube tonight and almost attacked the set. Catch you later."

"Hello, Kimberly, Tom Downing. Some women's group phoned the station, wants to know if you'll do a talk about women in TV. They'll pay, *modestly*, of course. Wanted to know if you were the same Kimberly Wells who used to be on Channel Eleven in Sacramento. Talk to you in the morning. Hope you had a nice time at Jacovich's party. The son of a bitch didn't invite me."

"Your father is going to kill me for phoning again." Mother once more. Kimberly groaned. "But he's asleep and won't know until the bill comes. Your ex-husband—would you believe that—came by this afternoon wanting your new phone number. Which I didn't give him, of course. Although I must say, he seemed so sad. Anyway, don't forget your father's birthday is next Monday. Honestly, Kimberly, I hate talking into this thing . . ."

One last message. "Kimberly, you really are an asshole." It was Richard's voice on the tape.

Kimberly switched off the electronic device. Tired now and feeling tearful, she flopped onto her bed. It had been a long and daunting night and she was not yet sleepy, nor did she want to stay awake, accompanied only by her thoughts. Try as she did to stop thinking about what Jacovich had to say, acid fumes filled all the passages of her mind.

As a youngster, a young girl, a young woman, her beauty had been elicited, fostered, praised, cultivated. If only she sprayed Arrid Extra Dry on her armpits, used Revlon on her lips, Clairol on her hair, Lysol in her toilet, Estee Lauder on her skin—if only she did all these things, she would be lovely and beloved and have the perfect life.

And she'd done all these things and what had it got her? A job displaying—Jacovich's harsh words came back—tits and ass.

And that's all they wanted from Kimberly Wells. If there was more to Kimberly Wells, let her keep it to herself. They were paying her for tits and ass. Period.

Christ! She wanted to cry. But wouldn't. Because that's what *they* expected her to do. They expected her to break down and be pitiful and she refused. You will not, she told herself in a hoarse stage whisper, cry, goddamnit. You will not!

There were times when she hated men. Not as individuals, but the system, the web of men.

Was this the end of the line, she wondered. Did she go on playing the cutie-pie news reader until the new cutie-pie waltzed into the station, as inevitably she would? Would she then be retired to some office job or simply canned as excess? Did she have any choice in the matter? Was there, for God's sake, anything that she could *do?*

Yes, she told herself, for a start, she could get rid of that stupid goddamn turtle, the stink of which reached her even where she lay. Ridiculous, she thought, to pay all this money for a pad smelling of turtle shit.

As for the rest, she thought wearily, there was nothing she could do but keep on trying. Hang in there, she told herself. It isn't too likely but it is possible that you'll get your chance to be something other than a popsicle.

With that, she pulled the quilt up over her shoulders, thought the hell with the lights, the hell with brushing her teeth. It sure would be nice to have a man to hold and a man to hold her, someone to keep her warm. The thought trailed off and mercifully, she fell asleep.

For Jack Godell, in his own apartment, many miles away on the arid outer reaches of the vast Los Angeles basin, there was no sleep, merciful or otherwise. Godell, shoeless, tousled, in a T-shirt and undershorts, sat holding an empty beer can, staring at a dark TV set in a silent apartment. He'd been sitting that way for an hour or more, ever since the late, late show had ended and he had arrived at a stage of weariness far beyond sleep.

His mind seemed to be divided into two distinct and separate hemispheres, each part dealing with a different time frame and a different set of data. One portion of his mind turned over slowly, reviewing his entire professional life, his personal goals, his beliefs in nuclear power, his devotion to science and technology. The other part of his mind was focused on the present, on trivia, it seemed. And it was maddeningly irrelevant.

He noticed, for example, how the strip of plastic base molding was beginning to separate from the corner of his wet bar. And where the plastic had separated, he could see the shabby edge of plywood, uncovered by rosewood veneer. Crappy construction, he thought—contact cement. Why the hell hadn't they added a couple of staples, it would have held the stuff together. He sighed. The apartment was only three years old and already it was coming apart.

He felt something like a click in his brain as the two hemispheres suddenly synchronized, turning at the same speed. My life is coming apart, Jack thought.

The thought was so clear, so insistent, that he said it aloud. Why not? There was nobody else in this 3 AM apartment. "My life is coming apart." He spoke the words slowly and then shuddered. The voice was his but it might have been a stranger's.

Aware now that he was falling into some kind of a psychological stupor, a kind of quicksand of introversion, he forced himself to review what he thought of as "the facts."

Fact number 1, he told himself, holding up his thumb. Something went on at that goddamn plant, something he couldn't explain, couldn't even get a handle on. Oh, sure, they'd gotten things under control. Oh, sure, they'd managed to get past the NRC investigation. But there was still something awfully WRONG.

And fact number 2? He paused for a moment. It was his baby, his ship; it was up to Jack Godell to find out what was going on. O.K., O.K., he told himself, quite freely talking aloud by now. That much is clear and that much I can handle.

But then you run into fact number 3. And that, Godell whispered aloud, is the goddamn company. Where did they stand? What attitude would they take? And he knew goddamn well where and what: save money, minimize costs and keep things looking good for the stockholders.

He sighed again and contemplated getting another beer. There were a couple of drops left in his empty can, tasting like liquid aluminum and he contented himself with that.

Nuclear reactors had become his career, his passion, his life. As a bright young submarine officer, he'd been one of the lucky ones, accepted as a trainee in the very beginning of the nuclear submarine program. It had seemed to him at the time that he had won a rare prize, had gained entry to a small and very precious place. There wasn't any doubt in his or any other submariner's mind that nuclear subs were the beginning of a whole new age of undersea warfare. More than that, they were the last best hope for the ultimate defense of the West.

He'd made the team, risen in its ranks and had acquired a bank of experience which gave him a kind of solidity and confidence he'd never known before. Jack Godell actually *felt* solid. When he walked into a conference room jammed with admirals or civilian experts, he actually felt the weight of his experience. It was like being a safe. He, Jack Godell, felt like a small, heavy cast-iron safe, packed with data, documents and know-how.

Which was how he got his job with C.G.& E. They were looking for him, not the other way around. Ex-service buddies of his, moving out into the civilian world, had spread his name around. C.G.&E. made him an offer he had to accept. But they wouldn't have made that offer if they hadn't recognized that confidence, that solidity, that quiet self-assurance he had felt right down to his toes.

And now? Now it was all shaken. All threatening to come apart. Who the hell *is* Jack Godell? he asked himself. And what the hell does he know?

The Ventana plant had been built according to NRC specs. It had been tested, examined, investigated and retested every step of the way. He knew the routine backward and forward and knew that every conceivable hazard would have been anticipated and corrected.

Of course, he'd also been in the service long enough to know that civilian contractors did not always deliver quite the product that the Navy had ordered. He'd seen enough sub-standard equipment, all the way from guided missiles to canned spaghetti, to know that greed, carelessness, indifference or stupidity had a way of slipping into the hold.

So even though it was unthinkable that the plant had been constructed with some sort of inherent defect, he knew what every veteran sea-dog knows: in time of trouble, and when all else fails, you damn well better start rethinking the unthinkable.

Still, the whole process wracked him. God knows he'd had his battles—in bars, cocktail parties, at university seminars. Always the same line-up. The uninitiated, the lay people, scared out of their wits by nuclear power, hysterically crying: cease and desist! And on the other side, a small, quiet band of people like Jack Godell—physicists, engineers, technicians—men who knew what they were doing, men who knew the importance of taking calculated risks.

Calculated. Sure, there were risks. But calculated. Calculated by some of the finest brains in the world, and minimized. There were risks in everything. Crossing the street. Eating canned tuna. There were risks in nuclear power as well.

But Jack Godell, along with the other members of that small, select band, believed the risks were worth it. More than that: he believed that he was, despite the opposition, contributing something to the future of mankind which would one day be regarded as vital . . . as vital as the sun. Energy. Without it, we go back to the caves. Except—Jack tossed his empty beer can across the room and tried to hit the sink. It fell to the floor with a clatter. Except—he added—we got a lot more people than we got caves.

He stared at his hands and saw that they were steady. Not bad, he thought. Not bad for an old fart who drinks and smokes too much and sits up worrying until three in the morning. So. The hands were all right. And the head was working pretty good.

Then what the hell was he worrying about? And his mind threatened to split up into separate hemispheres again. What it all boiled down to was that there was something rotten at the bottom of that plant. And all this brouhaha about the future of nuclear energy was beside the point. Somebody had to get his ass in gear and probe this matter. Really probe it until he found the soft spot, the danger area.

And that's you, Jack, he told himself. Little Jackie Godell. You better find that trouble zone —before it finds you.

If you're good enough, he added. Smart enough. If you aren't over the hill.

This last thought brought a smile to his lips and also brought him tiredly to his feet. So that's where it's been all along, he told himself. Not only have I been worried about this goddamn problem, I've been worrying about whether I can handle it!

Christ! he laughed. Physics is one thing, technology is another. But never forget that these are just tools in the hands of human beings. And human beings—well, they're human beings. Instead of worrying about technical matters, or the costs of construction, or the possibilities of a nuclear accident which could wipe out a large chunk of southern California, here is Jack Godell sitting in his living room in his underwear, worrying if he can still get it up again.

Yawning, he shuffled over to the kitchen and picked up his beer can, carefully placing it in the trash. Then he clicked off the lights and fell, exhausted, into bed.

FOUR

The Ventana plant lay in silence like some hulking, brooding, hibernating beast. It made the men edgy and uneasy; something vital had gone out of the center of their world. They moved back and forth without talking much, their expressions faintly troubled, their tempers tightly coiled.

Ted Spindler entered the control room cautiously, like a man coming home at three in the morning and trying to avoid a confrontation with his wife. He held up his ID to the guard at the desk without a word and started to move toward his console when a voice intercepted him.

"Ted, could I have a word with you?" It was Jack Godell calling through his open office door. Spindler allowed himself a moment's hesitation and a flicker of distaste. He did not want to go into Jack's office but there was no question that he must. Jack outranked him, and although Jack had never pulled that rank on him, he, Spindler, knew that Godell could and, if necessary, would.

He slouched into the office, flopped heavily on a chair and contemplated Godell, who was frowning at a mass of computer print-outs spread over the surface of his desk. Without raising his glance, Jack said, "Ted I'd like to get your impressions of one phase of our accident. Give a look over here, would you?" Godell's tone was easy, non-threatening.

Spindler heaved up and moved to the side of the desk.

"Right here," Godell said, pointing a finger to a print-out sheet. "About—let's see, fifteen seconds after the turbine trip. Do you recall—did you feel a secondary vibration?"

"Uh, yeah, main steam line closure."

"No," Godell said quickly. Perhaps a little too quickly. "That was here. Right at the start. I felt that too. I'm talking about a little later. More of a vibration, a shudder, I'd call it, than a shock."

Spindler pondered, tracing markings on the print-out with his index finger. "Probably this here, Jack. Relay valve number fourteen, automatically opening."

"Nnno," Jack said thoughtfully, "I don't think so. It was even after that. They didn't ask you about that? Not at all?"

Spindler shrugged. "They told us not to discuss the hearing procedure. Hell, you told me, yourself . . ."

"Don't do that to me, Ted. They meant during the investigation. Naturally. They want straight stories. They don't want guys together and covering up for each other. That makes sense."

"Is this part of the investigation?" Spindler's bulky body was stiff. He held himself a little away from the desk, his meaty shoulders bowed, his torso not fully erect. He looked, Jack felt, a little like a trained bear.

"What the hell's going on, Ted? What's wrong?"

"You know that as well as I do, Jack," Spindler said, unable to keep the wounded tone from his voice. "They had me in there seven hours. Seven goddamn hours. That's twice as long as anybody else. You and the other Navy boys have credentials, certificates for having completed this course, that school, this tour of duty and whatnot. Me, I'm just an old company man, been with this company since I got out of school. Twenty-five years. And you know and I know that I didn't know shit about nuclear stuff until they built this place and started training me. So I ain't got the papers, right? So you tell me, if there's a rhubarb, where do you think they're gonna point the finger? At the boys in blue? Come on!"

"Hey, wait a minute. We're not boys in blue. We're all in the same—excuse me, for Christsake—boat. We all draw our paychecks from the same company. What makes you think they're looking for a scapegoat? This is a routine investigation. Frankly, I welcome it. I don't know about the company, they're mostly interested in dollars, but I, for one, would like to know what the fuck is going on and this is a way to find out. I should think that you'd—"

"You don't think they're looking to point the finger, eh?" Spindler said.

"No."

"Yeah, well Jack, I've been with this company longer than you. I know how they do things. It may not make any sense but it's the way things are. When something goes haywire, count on it, sooner or later somebody gets the axe. They want profits and they also want blood."

"Hey, Ted," Godell tried a gentle laugh. "Come on, I don't know if you've been getting too heavy into the chocolate ice cream, but for Christsake, man—"

"I didn't think you'd understand," Spindler said curtly. "Is there anything else?"

"No," Godell said, the smile fading. "I just thought maybe—" his voice trailed off as Spindler clumped disconsolately from his office.

The usual group of people were sitting around watching the monitors as Kimberly Wells interviewed a man who had trained his German shepherd to recycle aluminum beer cans by crushing them between huge jaws and depositing them in a plastic garbage can. Kimberly looked very bright, very pretty and had just the right tone of respect and levity to bring this sort of nonsense off well.

"Does Pablo have any favorite brand of beer can? Not that I want you to name it, but just tell us if—"

"No. He'll squash up anything, except he don't like cans with lipstick on 'em. You know, sometimes a woman will drink a beer and leave a smudge on it. Lipstick. He won't touch one of them."

"And tell me, Mr. Grackle, about how much

do you realize each week from Pablo's recycling efforts?"

"Well, it depends. After a heavy weekend in our neighborhood, he's out just about all day Monday and most of Tuesday morning, bringing back the cans, one can at a time. I guess it just about pays for his dog food."

And so on. The sort of thing that keeps America glued to its TV sets day after day.

Several minutes later, Kimberly was having make-up swabbed from her face when Mac Churchill arrived. He stood behind her, gripped her shoulder fraternally, not possessively, and asked, "You speak to Richard?"

"Not since yesterday morning," Kimberly said. "But we're supposed to get together tonight after six to do some more work on the specials. Why do you ask?"

"Well, because—" Churchill hesitated until the make-up man turned his back to reach for a towel, and then he whispered in Kimberly's ear. "That son of a bitch stole the film."

"Oh, no!" Kimberly mouthed, not quite saying the words.

"I just came up here from the vault. Mildred said that he came down there yesterday morning and said he needed the film. She didn't know what the film was, nobody had bothered to tell her there was a hold on it, so she gave him a release to sign. He scrawled a fake signature which she didn't bother to check and off he went. Wasn't until this morning when I went to make sure that the thing was locked up tight that we found out it was gone and

Mildred explained how. She's in tears. I'm gonna have to tell Jacovich."

"Oh, Mac, please—"

"Please, what? You expect me to put my job on the line?"

"Couldn't you wait just a little while? Let me find Richard, talk to him. We're old friends. And in a way I'm partly responsible for this, I brought him in."

"How are you responsible? Did you shoot the film? Did you swipe the film? What are you talking crazy for?"

"Please let me talk to Richard and get the damn thing back. He can ruin himself this way."

"You can sure say that again. Jacovich is already pretty damned sore and when he hears this—"

"As a special favor, Mac, two hours, no more."

A man popped his head through the door. "Kimberly," he said, "I'm on my way to the cleaners. You got your stuff together?"

Kimberly handed him a bundle of soiled clothing and then gave Mac a look. There was nothing more to say.

Nothing more to say, she thought, and also, no more time to lose. Richard's lunacy was putting her whole career on the line. Grabbing her purse and her jacket, she swung out the door and down the corridor, sprinting for the parking lot. She thought she could handle Richard—if she found him. She'd damn well find him, she thought. Then she blasted out of the lot.

And while a frowning, anxious Kimberly was fighting her way through downtown traffic, fifteen miles away, at the far end of Los Angeles County, a group of C.G.&E. employees standing outside their cafeteria, reading a company bulletin board, when Jack Godell and Ted Spindler came into the hall.

"Hey, you guys," someone called out to Spindler and Godell, "give this a read. Congratulations!"

Spindler reached the bulletin board a pace or two before Godell. He read aloud. "Operating personnel responded swiftly and professionally, etcetera, etcetera, and while some operator error was evident, and procedures were violated to some degree, the overall result was a swift containment of a potentially costly event!" He turned to beam at Godell.

Appreciative voices came from the crowd.

"Hey, I can dig it!"

"Let's hear it for control!"

"That means we'll be back on-line as soon as possible. No red tape or hangups."

But Godell, after acknowledging the enthusiasm with a quick smile, lowered his spectacles from his forehead and searched the bulletin carefully. His face was grave and his manner was less than totally assured. He had something in mind but whatever it was, there was no mention of it in the memo.

Half an hour later, Kimberly was riding up the elevator to Richard's top-story loft. As usual, she showed signs of her hectic schedule, hair a trifle wind-blown, her notebook out, her purse open and ready to spill. She walked to the one door on the floor. It was marked RICHARD ADAMS PRODUCTIONS.

She tried the knob, found the door open and walked into the large, spacious two-story loft. The place was broadly skylighted and madè a perfect photographer's studio. It was also perfectly clear that the place was empty. Well, not quite empty. Hector Salas was lounging on a waterbed, reading a paperback.

"*Que tal, chica?*" he called out.

"Hi, Heck, where's Richard?"

"*No se. Estoy solo.*"

"What do you mean you don't know! Damnit, Hector, don't do that dumb chicano routine now. This is important."

"I honest to God don't know where Richard is," Hector said, shuffling over to a movieola where he had been splicing some film.

"Hey, listen." He held up a length of film. "I started to work on the solar section. Richard has some really great shots of sun, real moody stuff. Want to take a look?"

"Shit!" Kimberly said bluntly. She turned to face Hector, hands on hips. Fleetingly, it occurred to her that she was reproducing a favorite stance of her mother. "Richard stole the film of the nuclear accident. Conned it out of Mildred or whatshername in the film vault. Now Mac Churchill knows about it and if I don't get to Richard fast, Don Jacovich is going to know about it and the whole thing is going to hit the fan. So level with me, Hector, for God's sake. Our jobs are at stake. *My* job is at stake."

He remained silent.

"Hector, please!" Kimberly implored.

"I can make a guess."

"Then, for God's sake, make a guess!"

"I think he might have gone back to that plant. So he could find someone to talk to, to explain that accident to him. That's all he's been talking about. Trying to find out exactly what happened. Mind you, that's only a guess. Hey, Kimberly, you know something? I think Richard's crazy. A little bit. Not all the time. But I think he's a little bit crazy."

"I wish it were only a little bit," she said, heading for the door. "And he called me an asshole. The asshole!" She was out the door before Hector could say anything else.

When she got out to the Ventana plant, there was no sign of Richard. The guard said he had not come to the plant. Moreover, it was very clear that Richard had as much chance of being let inside as a weasel in a henhouse. Plainly, Bill Gibson had laid down the law. She felt blocked, frustrated, but then she had an idea. Faking despair and laying on the weak sister routine, she asked the guard if there was a place nearby where she could get a drink. He allowed as how there was.

She reached Harmon's bar a little after six. By her reasoning, the men in the plant would probably stop off somewhere for a beer on their way home each night and this was the only bar for miles around. The parking lot was jammed and she had a feeling she was in luck. She parked the car and paused to freshen her make-up. Tucking her blouse tightly inside her waistband so as to make the best of what God had provided, she left the car and sauntered into the joint.

The first thing that assailed her was noise. It was obvious that some sort of a celebration was going on. This wasn't just an ordinary evening in the neighborhood saloon. Looking over the heads of people, she could see that the bar was packed, and that there were as many wives as husbands present. That, in itself, was unusual.

"What's going on?" She nudged a young man nearby, and was pleased to see that his eyes went round.

"Hey, aren't you whatshername on the six o'clock news?"

"That's right," Kimberly said pleasantly, "What's going on?"

"Oh, this crowd is mostly from the Ventana plant. We're kinda celebrating. We had a plant shutdown and it looks like we're gonna be back in business like maybe tomorrow. You know, it's kind of a big thing for us."

"Sounds great," Kimberly said. "Congratulations." As she pushed her way a little closer to the bar, she could see that the place was really very crowded and also that there was no sign of Richard in the room. She could make out a form at the far end of the bar, however, surrounded by a cluster of people, and she realized that she was looking at the man she'd seen running the control room, the man she had on film.

Making her way through the crush, she reached the far end of the bar, took a good look around and confirmed the fact that Richard was nowhere in sight. She glanced over at Jack Godell and found that he was glancing back.

"Looking for someone?" he said amiably.

"Yes," she said, "looking for a friend of mine."

"Well, take it from an old hand, sit down and have a drink and if you sit in Harmon's long enough, sooner or later your friend will pass through. He's got to. Harmon's is the only halfway decent watering hole this side of Cahuenga Pass."

"The guard at the visitor's center told me that," Kimberly said. "I figured this must be it. But it looks as if my friend hasn't found it."

"Oh? Your friend work at the plant? Maybe I know him. I'm one of the crew over there. Actually, most of these folks either work there or are married to people who do."

Harry The Mix came up to Jack and smiled at Kimberly.

"What'll you have?" Godell asked.

"Uh, tap beer? Lovely."

"Coming right up, ma'am," The Mix said. "Saw you on the six o'clock news tonight. Let's see, it's now a quarter after six. How'd you get here, by rocket?"

"That was a taped segment," Kimberly said. "I think we shot that the other day."

There was a burst of raucous laughter and the sound of cheering. Godell peered out around Kimberly's flank to the dance floor where Ted Spindler was whirling his wife, Alma, around in an old-fashioned lindy. "Hey lookit Spindler go," Jack called out. "Do it, man, do it!"

"Looks like a big party getting off the ground," Kimberly said. "What's happening."

"Oh," Jack smiled. "Like I said, just about everybody here works at the plant. We had to shutdown this morning but we just got a clean bill of health."

"Really? The investigation's over so soon?"

"Yeah," Jack said. "You sound surprised."

Kimberly hesitated, then decided to lay her cards on the table. "Well, I was in the plant, in the visitor's gallery when that accident happened. I was looking right down on your control room."

Godell's voice was firm. "There was no *accident.*"

Kimberly flushed before his direct gaze. There was something about this man, about his unmistakable quality of authority that prompted her nerves to apologize. "I—I'm sorry," she fumbled. "I used the wrong word. Unanticipated transient, it said on the wire copy I read this morning. What was the cause, has that been worked out?"

"Yep," Godell said easily. "It's all on the public record now. Or will be. We had a faulty relay in the generator circuit. Am I making sense to you? If I said we had a fermin on the coristan, would that do just as well?"

"You're right," Kimberly laughed. "I hardly know how to plug in my hair dryer. A faulty what?"

"A faulty ten-dollar part that protects the generator. Let's not get technical."

"You mean it protects the generator when it works."

"Right. And for ten dollars it ought to work."

"Hmf," Kimberly said. "So that's what all the activity was about?"

"Well—that and also a stuck valve. No big deal though."

"Whew! You could have fooled me," Kimberly said. "Was it—I mean—was it ever dangerous?"

Godell paused and took a careful sip of his drink. Then he took a long and careful look at Kimberly. "No," he said finally. "You read the report. You saw that there was no mention of radiation, anything that might affect the public. Oh, here's your beer. Harry brought it all the way from Milwaukee in his pick-up truck."

"Get off my back, will ya, Godell. I'm runnin' around like a mad man—hey, that's on the house, folks. Mr. Harmon, that's the boss over there, he's takin' care of it."

Jack smiled and nodded in the direction of Harmon who immediately came over and gave Kimberly an enthusiastic handshake. "Welcome to our place," he said. "You're terrific, little lady. The wife and I watch you every night and the wife catches you live at noon."

"Thank you," Kimberly said, "and thanks for the beer."

"Hey, Jackie boy," a waitress pinched Godell on the ear. "Your dinner's sittin' over there on the table waitin' for you. Better go and eat before you get too smashed to walk."

"Rhoda, nag, nag, nag," Godell said.

"Hey, don't I know you from—oh, my God, it's Kimberly Wells," the waitress said. "You look just like you do on TV. What're you doin' with this creep? You know what you can get from these ex-Navy guys? Nothin' is what you can get."

"Hey, care to join me?" Godell said, picking up his drink and sliding off his bar stool.

"All we got is burgers and fries, honey," the waitress said. It was a gesture of sisterhood, giving Kimberly a chance to back off.

"Sounds good to me," Kimberly said, acknowledging the waitress's intent with a luminous smile.

Later, while Kimberly attempted to negotiate an enormous and sloppy hamburger, Godell looked on with a mixture of amusement and pleasure. She was good to look at, this girl, good to look at, good to talk to, good company for dinner. He wondered if there could be more. From some distant recess in his being, a locked closet in a forgotten hallway, came an answering chime—like a ghost clock tolling in the night. He'd forgotten he was capable of this kind of response, was surprised to be overtaken —by what? Desire? Involvement? Jesus! He thought he'd buried all that eons ago.

He slapped the ketchup bottle hard over his french fries to cover his consternation. Because his feelings were not totally clear. Yeah, sure, the kid was attractive all right, attractive and, he felt, in large measure compatible. But there was something else about her—some urgency, some need that caused him to keep his throttle low.

"Hey, this hamburger's a mess," Kimberly laughed, plucking lettuce shreds off her lip, "but it tastes marvelous."

"Enjoy," Jack said. "It warms my heart to see a young girl eat. If you finish everything on your plate, you can have ice cream for dessert."

"So when do you start cookin' again?" Kimberly asked.

"Me?"

"No," she laughed. "The plant."

"Oh. We'll probably go back on-line the day after tomorrow. Something like that. Why?"

Kimberly shrugged and mopped her chin with a fistful of napkins. "I was just wondering if the fact that there are safety hearings in process on the Point Conception plant prior to licensing, and the fact that that plant is owned by the same utility company—" she trailed off.

"Uh huh."

"Well?"

"You mean," Godell said, "because there's one hearing going on it might have a bearing on this one—cause them to speed up the investigation, get a clean bill of health so as not to jeopardize the Point Conception license? Is that what you're getting at?"

"Right. I could have phrased the question better, I suppose."

Jack shook his head. "Are you sure you came in here looking for a friend? You wouldn't be trying to pick me or some other plant person up just so you can get a story?"

"You've got it all wrong. I really was looking for a friend. And I'm not that kind of reporter. In fact, I don't even know your name. That tells you what kind of a reporter I am."

"Jack Godell. *Enchanté,*" Jack said, extending a hand.

"Kimberly Wells. Likewise, I'm sure."

They laughed and gulped beer.

"How about a game of rotation?" he asked.

"You're on." Kimberly lost no time selecting a cue and chalking it. Moving around the pool table, Kimberly displayed a skill Jack hadn't seen in a woman in some time. He also realized that it was quite a while since he'd been quite so fascinated by a derrière like that. As far as he was concerned, she could go on sinking balls all night.

"What kind of reporter are you if you're not *that* kind of reporter? What other kind is there?" he asked.

"Nine ball in the corner." Kimberly lined up her cue, not minding at all that Jack's gaze was fixed on her like a warm spotlight. "Attagirl," she sighed contentedly, as the nine ball trickled into the pocket.

"I can see that you had a misspent youth," Jack said, "hanging around pool rooms, improving your suntan. And of course I've caught your act on TV. You're not really a journalist, is that it? More of a what—performer?"

"Right on, brother," Kimberly said, lining up another shot. "Know what the boss calls me?"

"Unh unh."

"I'm the frosting on the cake. Shit!" she cried, as she missed her shot and scratched.

"I'm not partial to reporters," Jack said, lining up his shot.

"Why not?"

He carefully stroked the cue ball, sending the ten ball into a side pocket.

"Most reporters I've run into have the notion that the only good news is bad news. Calamity hounds. They give the nuclear industry a rough time. And face it, that's my business, my bread and butter. Every time there's a hiccup out at the plant, the news vultures come running, line up on the fence and start looking for corpses. Heyyyy! How about that!" He sank a long and difficult shot.

"I much prefer performers," he said, clicking off another crisp shot.

"Let me ask you a question," Kimberly said. "Assuming the public has a right to know, assuming that—if you'll pardon the sermonizing—an informed electorate is the cornerstone of democracy, can't you see that a reporter is a public servant? That he's working for the public good?"

"Should be," Jack said. "Should be, but most often, he's working to fatten his ass, advance himself personally. I guess I haven't met too many reporters who think of themselves as public servants."

"O.K.," Kimberly said, "let me try this on. Say I'm a reporter, a real reporter, a digger, investigator, right?"

"Right."

"Now, the question: was the public ever in

danger at any time during the accident at the Ventana plant? Excuse me for using the word accident again—but I think an investigative reporter would use it—to get at the truth!"

Godell paused and stared at her. Her face was firm and serious. There was no hint of banter now.

"All right, Miss Wells, let me tell you something," he said, laying his cue down carefully. "These plants are designed, almost to a fault, to anticipate accidents. The method is called 'defense in depth.' Not just back-up systems in case something malfunctions, but back-up systems for the back-up systems. Men have spent months, years, trying to imagine every conceivable thing that could go wrong—and I mean everything. From human errors to earthquakes to ice storms to termites, mice gnawing at insulated cables, rust, fungus, barometric changes and combinations of all of these things in every possible permutation.

"As each plant is being built, every single weld, every structural member, every single nut and bolt—I'm not talking about the toilet seats or the Coke machine—but everything that has to do with basic construction is X-rayed, spectrographed, whatever. It has to be approved and signed off by the construction company. We're talking about billions of dollars and that's just one reason why it's so expensive. But you better believe it's also safe. Checked, double-checked, triple-checked."

"Speaking of performers—" Kimberly said.

"What?"

"Well, you've just delivered an impassioned

little speech but you've also avoided answering the question."

"You really do go after it, don't you," Jack said, with a mixture of admiration and mild annoyance.

"I'm playing investigative reporter."

"O.K., everything that man does involves some element of risk. If he stays in bed he can get bed sores. If he puts on his hat he can go bald. If he drives a car he can kill himself. If he eats a chicken, for God's sake, he can get an overdose of hormones or a bone in his throat. Risk is the price you pay—"

"Crap!" Kimberly said succinctly. "You're still not facing the question. Was there any danger to the public—"

"None," Jack said, putting his cue stick up on a rack.

"None at all?"

"At all," Jack echoed. "You ready for a brandy? I am."

Kimberly hesitated. She felt a sudden remorse. She'd been enjoying herself, she realized. Liking this man, this dry and cagey but somehow trustworthy man. And she had, without thinking much about it, fallen into a kind of boy-girl mood, happy to move along with that current and see where it took them. But there was grit somewhere, something grated, something caused her feet to scrape bottom.

"I'd really like to, Jack, but I ought to get back."

"Ought to or have to?"

"Have to, really. Work I've still got to do tonight. And I have to be up early tomorrow.

I'm covering the street demonstrations outside the Point Conception hearings so that I can do it live on my twelve o'clock spot. Can I take a rain check?"

"Sure," Jack said. "But why don't you just stay up in this part of the woods instead of going all the way back to town? From here, you're half way to Point Conception."

It was, Kimberly knew, as close to an invitation to spend the night at his house as she would get. It was both direct and skillfully oblique and she appreciated that.

"I know it makes sense, but I've got a speech to write for next week and all the material is on my desk. My time is pretty carefully plotted and this is my night for homework."

He shrugged. "And you've still got to look for your friend, right?"

"I almost forgot. Thank you very much. I mean for the booze, the food. I liked it, Jack."

He grinned. "Y'll come back and see us, heah? And when you plug in your hair dryer, you can think of me."

"To say nothing of my electric can opener," Kimberly said slyly.

"You must have been reading my mind," Jack said. He laughed. "Good night."

" 'Night. Thanks again."

Jack watched her go out the door, also noticing the small bouquet of admiring glances she collected as she left. He sat down heavily at the table and, as the waitress moved by with a pot of coffee, he held out his cup.

"Gimme another shot of that, will you, Selma?"

"Sure—" she started to pour coffee but at that moment, something caused the table to jiggle and the coffee cup slid off the surface and crashed to the floor.

"Be right back," she said, going off to get another cup and a mop.

Jack picked up a few jagged pieces of the broken cup and stared at them. He was instantly sober, he realized, and startled. Something, somewhere, was terribly wrong.

At the same time, in the kitchen of a small attractive cottage, not far from the University of Cal., Santa Barbara, Richard sat across the table from a tall, lanky, bearded man who had fallen into a silence. A half-gallon jug of good red table wine was on the table between them and they had been sipping the stuff from mugs.

Finally, the man broke his silence. "What it came down to," he said softly, "what it always comes down to sooner or later in life is what the novelists call a crisis of conscience." He smiled faintly at Richard and then resumed talking to his wine mug.

"I had a career, a doctorate, recommendations —you know." He gestured. "I mean I could have carved out quite a future for myself in the AEC. But I just couldn't get past the evidence." He now looked up and his eyes were level with Richard's eyes and very steady.

"Don't get me wrong. I'm not special. Other men, good men, some not so good, have done the same thing. And they all had to face the same problem I did. They had to think what it would be like to become the devil's advocate, or, doubting Thomas or voice of dissent—whatever the hell you want to call it. Christ, nobody likes to cry doom. Nobody likes to say no. But—" His voice trailed off.

"But," Richard finished the sentence, "you felt you *had* to."

The bearded man nodded. "Something like that." He glanced around at the neat kitchen. There was order in the room, signs of moderate prosperity, signs of a woman's ongoing and affectionate care, children's drawings tacked up on the refrigerator door. "I'm lucky," he added. "As you can see, I haven't done too badly. Some of the dissenters have been so viciously attacked that they've been unable to get a decent job. The university, colleagues here, they've been very good to me. Even if they don't share my views, all of them. Very decent. And the head of the department sees to it that I get the time I need to go on with my dissent."

"For which," Richard said, "thank God."

The bearded man didn't smile. He shrugged. "Don't thank him too soon," he said. "More wine?"

Richard watched as he filled his mug. He was glad he'd come. Although he hadn't actually met Dr. Elliot Lowell until now, he'd heard of him often enough. Lowell had won a fair-sized reputation on the West Coast for his role as an "intervener," a man who appeared at hearings held by the Nuclear Regulating Commission to protest the licensing and construction of a nuclear power plant.

Richard's own role as a protester, dissenter, voice of opposition, had brought him into contact with so many "aroused citizens" that on walking into Lowell's living room earlier in the evening, he felt an immediate shock of recognition. What he hadn't quite been prepared for was Lowell's background, his credentials. As a top physicist in the AEC, as a brilliant theoretician, he was well-known in laboratories all over the world.

Still, he was humble, straightforward, earnest. And a deeply troubled man.

"As you know," he went on, "I have a couple of kids. You met them earlier." He paused. "I worried about that. And my wife was a problem. She was even more reluctant than I was. But, finally—we got past that. You have to. You have to respond to your instincts—even when your reason and your brain tell you that your instincts are—or could be—futile."

"Raising kids, you mean?" Richard said.

Lowell nodded. "Hell, continuing to propagate the race. Coming from where I do, knowing what I do, it's not merely a legitimate question, it's agonizing. But still—" He shrugged again.

"Do you regard your kids as a gesture of affirmation?" Richard asked.

"Gesture? Hell, no. They're kids. We're human, Janet and I. We go on hoping. We wouldn't be human if we didn't. We go on hoping that somehow the worst won't happen, that somehow things will get better, that people will come to their senses. As a scientist, I have to admit—in a general way, of course—that man has shown an astonishing gift for adaptation, a remarkable instinct for survival. So far."

"So did dinosaurs," Richard said.

"Dinosaurs didn't invent nuclear physics," Lowell said, smiling. "It's too early to know whether that's good or bad. In any case, it's what we've got to live with."

"Getting back to that film," Richard said, "based on what you saw, do you think you can make a strong case before the NRC? Can you get them to investigate Ventana?"

Lowell shook his head. "In some ways that film creates more problems than it solves. First of all, although it certainly *looks* as if you photographed a near-disaster, I can't be quite confident about it. We'll leave that question to Greg Gilbert who'll see it in the morning. He's worked in a control room like that. He knows those procedures backward and forward. I don't. I'm much more of a theoretical person than a nuts and bolts person."

"Yes," Richard pressed, "but you're the one with the standing, the credentials. When you go before the NRC, these guys have got to listen."

"Well, they listen, all right," Lowell said. "After all, they're pretty competent men, some of them. But whether or not they'll convince all that easily—that's another question."

"But they've *got* to see—"

Lowell held up a hand. "I hope you realize that if you do manage to project that film, you're opening yourself up to arrest and possible sentencing. You understand that, don't you?"

"Hell, I've been there before," Richard said.

"And the second thing is, that film, indicative as it may be, is only that, indicative. It indicates a possible problem, it doesn't define it. It isn't quite the evidence I'd like to have."

"Christ, what do they want—Hiroshima?"

"Please remember," Lowell said dryly, "I'm on your side. I regard the construction, dissemination, proliferation of nuclear devices—of any kind—an absolute danger to the future of life on this planet. I think any and all nuclear activity should be stopped until it can be demonstrated scientifically that there are adequate safeguards for the disposal of nuclear waste and adequate protective methods for the maintenance and operation of nuclear devices. Now, that's my basic position in a nutshell—so you know where I stand."

Richard found himself a little embarrassed. "Of course, I know that. I only—"

"I'm also a scientist dealing with other scientists," Lowell said, "and I have to proceed in an orderly, an intelligible way. Your film is dramatic. And possibly Greg Gilbert will find something in it that I've overlooked. But it *still* doesn't show, beyond any question of doubt, that there is something abnormal at Ventana. It only indicates there *might* be."

Richard pondered this for a moment. He was tired. The hour was late. It had been a long drive and he was feeling the effects of it. He was also feeling less certain of his position than when he had arrived.

"I guess the question is: will this be enough to get the NRC to open up that plant?"

Lowell spread his hands. "Anybody's guess. On the other hand, given my position, I've got no other choice but to try."

FIVE

The following morning, Jack Godell sat outside a massive steel door much like the door of a huge bank vault. He was seated on a short metal stool, awkwardly bending over to zip the fasteners on his anti-radiation boots. The bulky radiation suit he was wearing made it difficult to reach his toes and he was perspiring underneath the layers of lead-impregnated cloth. As soon as he was done, he stood up, put on his helmet and gloves, and picked up his flashlight and Geiger counter. Then, looking like a bright orange Martian and feeling vulnerable despite his protective cover, he activated a lever which opened the heavy steel door.

It swung silently, set in walls of ultra-thick concrete. Ahead of him loomed another door exactly like the one he'd passed through. Pausing, he locked the first door behind him and experienced for a moment the terror of entrapment. Shuffling ahead, he opened the second steel door and when that finally swung shut behind him, he was in the containment area. He'd been here before and each time he stood at the top of this huge eerie space, preparing to descend to the depths, he felt as if he had left the normal world.

The containment dome rose approximately ten stories from its lowest level, and as he stood on the small metal platform he could see all the way down this vast dark silo to the very bottom of the reactor core. There were no windows and the lights, though powerful at his level, grew dimmer and dimmer as he peered into the depths below.

Godell was not a fanciful man. His background was engineering, science and technology. Yet he could never come into this place without wondering if he was looking at a preview of hell.

Quickly, he checked his instruments to make sure they were working, and then began his long, slow descent down the spotless steel staircases. As he moved, he played his flashlight over the immense forms around him—pumps, three and four stories high, stainless steel pressure tanks as large as dirigibles, girders and pipes gleaming in the half-light of explosion-proof lamps. And everything vibrated with a deep, throbbing hum. He felt it in the handrails, in the metal plates beneath his feet. His body was alive with the energy coming from that deadly core far, far below him in the semi-darkness. He paused, took a few deep breaths in his special gas mask and then made his way downward again.

He forced his mind to concentrate on the things around him, refusing to think about the incident in the control room. Dutifully, he monitored the radiation as he went downward, falling back on training procedures as he used to do in the Navy. He would do it as a veteran officer should—strictly by the book.

As he got to the lowest level, an orange figure dwarfed by a forest of steel girders and immense concrete blocks, he removed and unfolded a blueprint from one of his suit pouches. The reflection from the overhead lights was too dim and he unhooked a flashlight from his belt. The flashlight too, started to falter and he cursed, shook it, and restored its light level. Satisfied that he was correctly oriented, he began touring the steel-and-concrete forest.

Suddenly, Jack's Geiger counter began to chatter nervously. He halted and played his light around into dark recesses as far as it would reach. He took a half-step forward. The Geiger counter sound was steady. Then, slowly, he pivoted on his heel. The Geiger counter was still steady, still high, but not yet alarming. Then he took another half-step forward and the Geiger counter crackled almost immediately into an unbroken, high frequency tone.

Sweating now inside his radiation suit, Jack was able to hear the sound of splashing water above the crackling of the Geiger counter. He flashed his light in that direction and saw the light glint off a pool. Then he swept his light downward and saw that his own boots were standing in an inch or so of black water.

He backed off instantly, retreating along the line he had come, attentive to the sound and indicator of his Geirger counter, which was quickly going back to normal.

"Christ!" he thought, "I'd better get the hell out of here—fast!"

Half an hour later, however, he was back down there again, this time accompanied by a five-man team of orange-suited dwarfs. They all had Geiger counters and flashlights and they were all grouped beneath a massive recirculation pump which rose two stories above them. The pump was raised above their heads on three giant legs, its outlet pipe running downward into the reactor core. And beneath this pump, just where they were standing, was a shallow sump filled with contaminated water. Their Geiger counters buzzed like maddened flies against a window pane.

De Young spoke loudly from behind his mask. "Martin, you get a crew down here and clean this up! Rusty, have your boys climb all over that pump. I want them to check every seal, every flange, rivet, nuts and bolts. Everything. And you stay right on top of them to make sure they do a thorough job. I don't want any man passing something up because he decides there's no way water could come out of that place. You decide, get me? It's your responsibility and I want your full report."

Rusty signified his acknowledgment by touching a gloved finger to his head.

De Young turned to look at Godell. "We're going to have to test it, Herman," Godell shouted through his gas mask.

De Young nodded agreement. "What do you recommend?"

"Well the sure way—tear that goddamn

pump down and give it a full, phase-by-phase inspection."

De Young shook his head. Even inside his bulky suit, his reaction was clear. "We can't do that," he shouted. "It'd keep us off-line for two weeks. That's over five hundred thousand a day in lost revenue. You're looking at ten million dollars. I can't justify that. Not yet."

He gestured and directed Jack's attention to a particular area. "It's obvious," De Young shouted, "the leak is coming from a recirculation seal. So we'll tighten the seal first and then check her out. But we don't take that pump apart until we have no other recourse."

Godell shrugged but the shrug was lost inside his orange spacesuit.

De Young turned to another man. "Put TV monitors on that pump and run her up to a hundred per cent of rated speed. That might tell us something."

Godell agreed. "It might—" he said dubiously.

"What?"

"I said it might," Jack shouted again.

"Okay, then let's get at it," De Young concluded. "We can test that thing as soon as we get the hell out of here. Everybody together?" They nodded.

When they were outside the outermost pressure door and had stripped the sweaty gas masks from their faces, De Young gave Godell a wan and troubled smile.

"Now," he said, "thanks to you, I've got to get on the horn and call downtown. And they're not going to like what I have to tell them. I'd already told them we'd be back on-line by three o'clock this afternoon."

"Thanks to me?" Jack said. He was not smiling.

"I'm only kidding, Jack. Lousy joke. Of course, thanks to you. You discovered the fault. I only meant—well, you know—the bearer of ill-tidings and all that. You've had enough experience with headquarters people to know that they don't want to be bothered by the facts. All they want is performance."

"Brass is brass," Godell agreed, "the world around."

As Herman De Young made his reluctant way to his office and the inevitable telephone call, Kimberly Wells, along with TV technician Tom Finley, was aloft in a helicopter heading for the Point Conception area.

"I think I can see Richard," Kimberly shouted into Tom's ear. "Isn't that Richard?" She pointed to a figure, accompanied by another figure, just getting out of a jeep near a group of demonstrators picketing outside the hearings.

"If it ain't, somebody's driving his jeep. No mistaking that rattletrap," Tom agreed.

Moments later, Kimberly and Tom got out of the chopper and made their way toward the KXLA van. The crowd of demonstrators was not yet large but it was steadily increasing as more and more vehicles drove up. Kimberly was gratified to see that they had banners and posters which would show up well on camera and that there was a fair amount of "color" already assembled. One group called itself MOTHERS FOR PEACE, and they had a fancifully dressed character labeled CAPTAIN PLUTONIUM. There were the usual bearded folksingers strumming guitars and a few people swathed in turbans and white robes.

Kimberly tapped Tom on the shoulder. "I'll be right back—"

"Hey, don't get lost, we've still got a lot of preparation," he warned.

"Right back," she repeated, and then strode quickly across the high school campus where the hearings were taking place. Inside the building, she looked around hastily for signs of Richard and moved to a doorway temporarily marked Atomic Safety and Licensing Board. Inside the board members were assembled around a table on a small stage at the front of the room. In the audience several dozen women were seated and one of them, on her feet, held a statement in trembling hands, from which she read: "To the Atomic Safety and Licensing Board, these are pictures of children we love."

It was apparent that this woman was not accustomed to public demonstrations. Yet her passion had caused her to forsake her privacy and risk public display. Kimberly made a mental note to check her as a possible interview later on.

Another woman rose and began handing batches of 8x10 glossy photos to the members of the board.

Her voice quavering, the first woman continued.

"Since the children themselves cannot be here, nor can all of them tell you of their deepest fears, we ask that you consider them when you make your decision."

Kimberly could not spot Richard anywhere in the room.

Another woman rose. "Those children and others like them will be the ones who will inherit the consequences of your—and our—actions. Remember the word 'safety' in your title. Radiation is *not* healthy for children and other living things."

There was a chorus of "Right on's" and a vigorous spatter of applause.

This speaker began reading the names of the children on the photographs and giving their ages. Kimberly, craning to discover a sign of Richard, finally caught a glimpse of a ragged sleeve passing the open door. She got up quickly, excusing herself as best she could, and raced back out to the corridor. She saw what she was certain was Richard, accompanied by another man, just turning off the corridor.

Springing quickly down the hall, she finally caught up to them. "Richard! For God's sake!"

Richard turned to face her, smiling slightly, then said a word to the man with him, who immediately moved away.

"Hey," Richard said, squeezing her arm, "didn't you get my message?"

"What message, for Chr—"

"I left a message for you on your phone-gizmo."

"Yes, I got your message. Or no, I don't

remember. Anyway, where the *hell* have you been and what the hell have you been up to?"

"Look, Kimberly—what you don't know won't hurt you, okay?"

"It is *not* okay! What I don't know could not only hurt me, it could kill me. Where's that damned film? And don't give me that 'what film' look. They know you took it. Mildred down in the vault told Mac Churchill. So you've got to give it back, is that clear? And you'd better hope that Jacovich doesn't turn this over to the police. If he hasn't already done so."

"Kimberly, for God's sake—" It was a breathless Tom Finley, clutching at her arm. "Hurry, will you. We're running out of time."

"Wait!" she kept her eyes on Richard. "I have to talk to you, Richard. This is serious."

He just grinned and started moving off to his former companion. She glanced back at Tom and gave him a reassuring wave.

"Richard!" she called. "Where are you going to be? I've got to—"

Richard just waved blithely and kept on walking.

I've got no choice, Kimberly thought desperately. My job is on the line. His neck. My job. She turned and raced back to Tom.

Kimberly's coverage of the hearings was being fed live to TV stations all over southern California. One of the TV sets tuned to her broadcast was, not surprisingly, in the cafeteria of the Ventana nuclear energy plant.

Jack Godell, carrying his tray, moved up to a small knot of employees who were watching the telecast. He paused, forgetful of his food, to watch the set.

Kimberly was on camera, looking as good or perhaps better than he recalled, thrusting a microphone up to the mouth of a serious looking young mother who said, "What about posterity? Doesn't anybody care about that word any more? Does anybody remember what it means? Posterity is a concern for those who aren't yet born. For future generations. Some of mankind's most heroic and noble acts have always been made in the name of posterity. Now, it appears, we're leaving posterity tons and tons of poisonous nuclear waste. What a dreadful gift!"

As Jack watched the set and listened to the interchange between Kimberly and various people she was interviewing on camera, some of the brasher spectators were ad-libbing their own live exchange with the figures on camera.

"Hey, baby, whattaya gonna do for heat this winter?"

"How're the little bastards gonna watch Captain Kangaroo?"

That brought a laugh.

"Yeah, and what about jobs, folks? How do I take care of *my* family and *my* kids without my job at the plant?"

That brought a chorus of angry approbation.

Drawn back to reality again by the voices of his co-workers, Godell realized his lunch was getting cold. Grimacing faintly to acknowledge the total irony of this situation, he moved away from the TV set to take his lunch in a quiet corner. Everybody thinks about number one, he told himself. I'm worried about my lunch. Those guys, about their jobs. The mothers, about their kids.

But, wait a minute, he told himself. Those mothers weren't just worried about *their* kids, but also about kids unborn. And unborn kids of those unborn kids. And the truth is, Jack thought, I ain't so comfortable about that myself. And there were other things he wasn't so comfortable about, he realized. He wasn't so comfortable about having Kimberly flash through his life like a bright, curvy comet and then leave, just as quickly as she had appeared. And finally, he wasn't at all—not the least bit—comfortable about the way this pump investigation was going. It was a makeshift operation that might, if they were lucky, reveal the fault, but could also cover up some hidden defect until it was too late. He stirred his minestrone thoughtfully and decided he wasn't hungry any more.

The heavy window shades in the high school classroom had been drawn so that the room was darkened. A movie projector had been set up at the rear of the room and a film was being shown on a small screen at the front. Two men attended the projector and Richard sat nearby. They all looked up as Kimberly opened the door and called out, "Richard!"

"She's O.K.," Richard said, gesturing for Kimberly to enter.

She moved quickly to his side and sat down, hissing in his ear, "Richard, you're *not!* You *wouldn't* run that film! My God, this is all we need! Do you realize that you've not only committed a crime, you've compounded it by—"

"Ssh!"

"Who *are* these men?"

"One," Richard whispered, "is Dr. Elliot Lowell, a physics professor and what they call an intervener, I mean a guy who gets up at these hearings and speaks for the opposition. And the other is a nuclear engineer, I mean a guy who really knows the ins and outs of generator construction. The other is Greg Gilbert. He used to be in the control room of a nuclear generating plant."

Kimberly looked up at the screen. There was no doubt about it, the film was the one that Richard had made when they were in the control room. In spite of herself, the footage fascinated her. It was remarkably good considering that it had been shot from the hip. And it was also shocking insofar as it recalled the urgency and drama of those moments she had lived through.

Finally, the film ended with a small clatter and a burst of white light filled the screen. The man whom Richard had identified as Dr. Lowell got up and switched on the lights in the room.

"When I saw this footage last night, I thought we'd better show it to you, Greg. You're in a better position to analyze it because you're familiar with the technology and the equipment."

"Well," Greg said, "these set-ups are pretty

much standard. I've put in a lot of time in a control room just like that one."

"So what's your view?"

Greg shrugged and smiled self-effacingly. He glanced at Richard and then at Kimberly, almost as if he were embarrassed at what he had to say. "I guess I'd have to say—from what I've seen up there on the screen—you people are probably lucky to be alive. Mind you, I can't be certain. There's a lot more information—but still. Looking at it raw like that, yeah, lucky to be alive. And that goes for a fairly large chunk of southern California."

Kimberly felt something heavy fall to the pit of her stomach. She turned to look at Richard and found his eyes looking steadily, unwaveringly into her own. She was speechless.

Greg turned to Dr. Lowell. "Hey, Elliot, do you think we might run it one more time? There's something back there I'd like to look at again. Maybe I can tell you where and you can stop the projector. O.K. with you people?"

Richard nodded and gestured. Kimberly found herself still unable to speak or, for that matter, to move.

The film was quickly rewound, the lights were turned off, and the camera started forward again. Kimberly found herself, through the lens of Richard's camera, staring intently once again at that control room.

In that very control room at Ventana the same people as before were gathered again. TV monitors had been switched on, giving filmed closeups of the malfunctioning pump. Godell and Spindler were watching the monitors with Herman De Young just behind them. Elsewhere throughout the room, various technicians were at their standby positions, monitoring other controls.

"It's up to ninety-five per cent rated speed," a technician called out.

De Young peered at an instrument and then back at the TV set. He leaned close to Jack Godell's ear and said softly. "Steady as a rock, so far."

Godell didn't answer. His expression was enigmatic. "Take her up to one hundred per cent," he called out to a technician.

"Roger, one hundred per cent of rated speed."

Flipping his spectacles into place, Jack moved quickly to another bank of gauges and lighted indicators and Spindler did the same. Then they moved back to the TV monitor showing the live functioning of the pump. Herman De Young followed them with a careful scrutiny of his own. All controls were functioning perfectly, a clear indication that the pump was performing normally.

Godell turned slightly toward De Young. "I think we ought to take 'er up over one hundred per cent to be on the safe side."

"But Jack," De Young answered, "we're at the top of the scale."

Jack gestured impatiently. "I've got a man stationed in diesel generator control. He can increase the frequency so we get 110 per cent out of the pump. We can follow it on the computer print-out. O.K. with you?"

De Young shrugged and then said clearly, "O.K."

"Barney," Godell called out, "you punch in the pump speed as it comes in. Sam?" Godell picked up a phone, "run it up another ten per cent."

Craning forward, they watched an indicator closely as the needle started to inch up. 101, 102. The TV monitor on the pump showed that it was working perfectly, steady rhythm, no water leaks. Godell checked his watch, then automatically confirmed it with the control room clock. After a while De Young's voice broke the tense silence.

"Okay, guys, it looks as if we were right. Tightening that seal corrected the malfunction. Take her back down to normal slowly and then completely off. I think we'll go back on-line this afternoon as we'd originally planned."

Godell picked up his phone. "Take her back down, Sam," he ordered. The room was suddenly filled with smiling men, exchanging mutually congratulatory pats. But Jack Godell wasn't smiling. And he didn't trust himself to look directly at Herman De Young.

Back at the high school at Point Conception, Kimberly listened intently as Greg, the nuclear reactor engineer, commented on the film that was unreeling before them. Her attention was not wholly focused on the engineer, however. A part of her mind kept returning to the evening before that she'd spent with Jack Godell. And she kept having the uneasy feeling that he'd told her less than the whole truth.

"Now this is a reactor SCRAM," Greg was saying. "What you're seeing on the screen right now. In a SCRAM situation the entire system operates automatically for ten minutes. And they're obviously having a problem. There, you see that?"

On-screen they could see Jack Godell move toward the core water level indicator.

"Good! Can you stop the projector right there?"

Richard stopped the film on a frame showing Godell and Spindler, both intently leaning forward to peer at the water level indicator.

"This is a problem that they have to deal with manually, not automatically," the engineer went on.

"It was a stuck valve of some kind," Kimberly said. "That's what Godell told me."

"Godell told you!" Richard was surprised. "When did you—"

"I went out there last night. I was looking for you. So I ran into Jack Godell and I recognized him—after all, I'd had a good chance to watch him in the control room. And he bought me a beer and a hamburger. With everything on it. And he said it was a stuck valve."

"On your hamburger?"

"Will you *ever* grow up?" Kimberly said testily.

"O.K., people," Greg resumed. "Whichever

valve stuck, it's forcing them to deal with the reactor water level. And from their behavior, their expressions, their movements, anyone can see that the situation is serious. In most control rooms, and I'm sure theirs is the same, the annunciators they're most concerned with are in the same area as core water level. I'm not sure, but they may have come very close to exposing the core."

"And if that's true," Lowell said, "we came very close to having a China Syndrome."

In the silence, Kimberly felt awkward asking the question, but still she needed to know. "What's a China Syndrome?"

"I'll answer that, Miss Wells," Lowell said. "If the core is exposed, for whatever reason, the fuel heats beyond core heat tolerance in a matter of minutes. Nothing can stop it. It melts then, right through the bottom of the core, the container, through the concrete basin and in fact, it melts right through the bottom of the plant. Remember your childhood myth? If you dig straight down and far enough, you'll get to China? Well, this is the same idea. Theoretically, that core could melt its way right through the center of the earth. But of course it couldn't actually, because sooner or later it would hit the water table. And when it did, the amount of steam generated by this incredible heat, would send a blast of vapor up through the rock and earth and into the atmosphere. Needless to say, that vapor would be intensely radioactive and it would move quickly up and away, depending on wind strength and direction. How many people would be killed? Hard to say. Possibly it might render an area the size of the state of Pennsylvania permanently uninhabitable. Well, let's say for 25,000 years. That's reasonably permanent. And I'm not yet talking about the number of cancer cases that would be showing up later. Within weeks, months and years after the blast. They could number in the hundreds of thousands, even millions."

"My God!" Kimberly gasped. "Is that true?" She was incredulous.

"Yes. Without being alarmist, it is theoretically entirely possible. In fact, highly probable."

"Theoretically," Kimberly said.

"Theoretically, to a scientist, means that the total event hasn't yet occurred but conclusions derived from laboratory experiments indicate a strong degree of probability. And one thing more: we have a mass of very hard data from Hiroshima and Nagasaki. That's something more than laboratory experimentation."

Kimberly swallowed and then said, half to herself, "And he told me we were in no danger at any time."

"I think that was a lie, Miss Wells," Lowell said. "And I think he knew it."

SIX

In the engineering records room of the Ventana plant, Jack Godell sat under a powerful fluorescent light at a high drafting table. On the table before him was a drawing of a section of the recirculation pump. Jack followed the contours of the drawing with his index finger and then, without moving his gaze from the drawing, allowed his hand to stray off, reach for a small pocket computer and punch some figures in it. He picked up the computer and stared at the results.

Impatient, he scrubbed out the result on the pocket computer and dropped it back on the table. The room was quiet and airless and his eyes stung. He rubbed his eyes and resisted an impulse to go home—or better still—go to Harmon's Bar and forget the whole thing. But he couldn't quite do that and he wasn't sure why. Call it professionalism, pig-headedness, whatever. He wasn't satisfied with the explanations he'd given himself. He was also aware, and more than aware, that he was probing in an area that might yield trouble, big trouble, and for himself. Herman De Young had made the official position clear: be thorough, but get back on-line as soon as possible. The company couldn't afford to lose revenue—not at $500,-000 per day.

So what's the point? Jack asked himself. The malfunction seemed to have been cleared up. The pump tested out well. De Young was off the hook. The company was happy. And Kimberly Wells could plug in her hair dryer. Kimberly Wells . . . that was another trouble spot. He hadn't been entirely straight with her. And while it might not have mattered, one wasn't always straight with every Tom, Dick and Harry, she wasn't any of those guys. She was a girl whom he had particularly liked. The first, in fact, for many years.

Damnit, he muttered to himself. Damnit, Godell, you're getting to be a senile old grouch, a man with an obsession.

Idly, he allowed his gaze to travel back across the drawing again and then suddenly, he sat up straight. He got off his stool and went to a bank of filing cabinets. Thumbing across drawers, he came to the right one, opened it, foraged inside and came up with a manila envelope. The envelopes, all suitably marked, contained X-ray negatives of the various machine parts indicated on the drawing. Jack placed one of these negatives over a light box and flicked on the switch.

Peering at the X-ray with a magnifying glass, he focused directly over a pipe weld, then scanned the lower left corner of the negative and saw the number 2233. He replaced that negative with one numbered 2234, and examined it in the same way. One after another, he drew X-ray negatives from the envelope and examined them with the magnifier. Then he stopped.

He sucked in his breath.

He reached for the first neg and put it back on the light box. Then he took the next neg and placed it on top. Down at the bottom of each negative, below the number, was the signature of the technician who had signed and approved them: D. B. Royce.

"My God!" Jack said, half-aloud. Then, louder, "Oh, shit!"

A quarter of an hour later, he caught up to Herman De Young who was moving through a deep corridor inside the plant. "Herman!" Jack called.

De Young stopped and turned, waiting for Godell to come up to him. Jack was breathing hard. "Herman, we got problems," he said.

De Young frowned, openly annoyed. He thought this crisis had passed, *wanted* it to be past. "What now, Jack? The pump checked out. You were there—"

"Static tests, Herman. They didn't tell us a thing."

"What do you mean, didn't tell us? You ran that thing up to 110 per cent of rated speed, for God's sake. If that doesn't reveal a weakness, what will?"

"Herman, listen to me. That test doesn't show us what will happen if we have to shutdown again to SCRAM at full power. Do you see? Any sudden jolt to the system—"

"But Jack, that's just—"

"Goddamnit, Herman, listen to me!" This

was a command, and it so surprised De Young that he turned around fully to stare at Godell. Both Godell and De Young were ex-Navy and both had an inbred respect for rank. In their present functions, De Young as plant manager clearly outranked Godell as shift manager. Yet Godell had seriously breached protocol. It was enough of an anomaly to cause De Young to stop in his tracks.

"I was going through the Quality Assurance Reports," Godell said, "and I found some irregularities in the contractor's documentation of the pump support structure. So I decided to check out the X-rays of the weldings. Here, see for yourself."

He started to hand the negatives to De Young, then thought better of it and held them up before a nearby light.

"Identical, Herman. You see that?" Godell said. "That's the same picture, over and over."

De Young let out suppressed breath. "My God, Jack. No contractor can possibly supply every stupid document the government calls for. So they didn't take all the pictures they were supposed to take? So what? And anyway, these X-rays are six years old."

"Right," Godell said crisply, "and so are those welds down there. Six years old."

De Young shrugged and handed the negatives back to Godell. "I don't see what all the fuss is about, Jack. I'm trying to be fair-minded about this thing . . ." His voice trailed off, lacking conviction.

"At the very least," Godell said, "I think we

should get new radiographic studies of the pump support structure. It's the safest way to check things out."

"Damnit, Jack, that's absurd. Do you know what you're talking about? Of course you know —fifteen, maybe twenty million dollars. Forget it. I mean, there's no way. What you'd better do, you'd better get back to the control room, start the mill up, turn it over to Spindler and then take the rest of the day off. And if you want, take tomorrow off too. I think you need a rest, Jack. I really do. Sometimes we get stretched in this business and I think you could use a little rest."

Jack nodded, his head bowed slightly, the X-rays held limply in one hand. It was difficult to tell from his expression whether he agreed with his chief or not. Maybe De Young was right; he had, indeed, felt stretched. And perhaps he did need a rest. But he couldn't escape the feeling that his recommendation had been denied and along with it, De Young had rejected the one possible means of finding out what was wrong.

Back in the control room, with the X-ray negatives safely restored to their jackets and a fresh cigar in one hand, a fresh cup of coffee in the other, Jack Godell gave a pretty fair imitation of his former self. He was the veteran sea dog, the old skipper returned to take over the bridge.

All the technicians were at their standby stations. Spindler, at his console, had his eye on Godell, the way the first violinist keeps his eye on the conductor. Jack gave Spindler a faint nod. He responded on cue:

"The reactor is on hot standby. The turbine is on turning gear. We've got a clear board, Jack."

Godell nodded, allowed his eyes to sweep the vast banks of light indicators and confirm Spindler's report. Everything was ready to go.

"Okay, fellas," Godell said softly, "follow normal sequence for rod withdrawal up to the top of the S.R.M.'s."

As if all the men in the room had been activated by a single and instantaneous impulse, they began to move handles, inspect dials, make notes on clipboards, and push control levers in and out. It was almost as if a whole room full of store window mannequins had come to life.

"Rods out to thirty per cent," Spindler called out.

Jack acknowledged with a nod in Spindler's direction and with a gesture to the other men. Steady as you go, his gesture said. And one by one, the various dials, meters, gauges, computers, oscilloscopes and all the other paraphernalia of the control room, sprang to quivering life. Far down in the bowels of the plant, they could feel a faint but rising throb as the immense turbines began to spin faster and faster.

On the following afternoon Jack Godell pulled his car up to the gate of the Point Conception construction site. He glanced around—

it was a familiar scene. The huge dome of containment rising over the bulk of the generating plant. Men in hard hats moving back and forth, skip loaders carrying sections of pipe, gardeners already tending the landscaping which had been completed the year before. This was a plant which, it was obvious, was very close to going on the line.

He passed through the gate after the usual security check and was permitted, by special courtesy, to drive his own car around to the rear of the plant. There he found, as he'd been told he would, a blue and white trailer, marked: FOSTER–SULLIVAN, QUALITY ASSURANCE. As he got out of his car, a white-collar worker in a hard hat leaned out the door, shouted something to another workman passing by and then withdrew. Jack presented himself at the open door and knocked lightly on the frame. A barrel of burning trash smoldered nearby.

The man in the hard hat looked up from a desk with a large light box on it. He'd been studying X-rays.

"Hi, you Royce?"

"That's right."

"I'm Jack Godell, shift supervisor at Ventana. I called this morning."

"Oh, sure, Jack. Come on in. What can I do for you? Care for some coffee? Help yourself."

Jack smiled and waved the coffee aside. "I guess you heard," he said, easing himself into a chair, "we had a bit of a problem over at our shop this week."

"Yeah, right. I did hear that. But I gather

you cleaned it up pretty fast. You're back on-line, aren't you? Or about to be?"

"Yeah," Jack said, rummaging in his brief case. He came up with a manila envelope and withdrew a sheaf of X-ray negatives. "I was checking the X-rays," he continued, "especially the welds on the pump support structure inside containment. I believe you signed these negs, didn't you? D. B. Royce?"

Royce took the X-ray film and spread them on the light box. "That's right. That's my signature. Go on."

"Well—" Jack hesitated. "It's the same shot. I mean those aren't different welds. That's the same weld shot over and over."

"Oh," Royce sounded a trifle relieved. "Those welds were all fine, there was no need—"

"How do you *know* they were fine?" Jack said. "You didn't X-ray them all."

Royce stood up and walked toward the door of the trailer, holding the X-rays up to the light. Just outside his door was a metal drum which had been used to burn construction trash. He gave a last look at the film, grunted, then dropped them into the barrel. The acetate film burst instantly into flame.

"Hey, what—" Jack protested. Then, "Never mind, there are a lot more where those came from."

Royce turned and his voice had an edge to it. "Everyone I checked was fine. Up to standard."

"Up to . . . Mr. Royce, we have no idea what those pump supports will do if they're hit with a sudden stress. We have no idea because we have no visual record of all the welds. Now that pump is one of the two water coolant pumps that keeps the core covered. What I'm saying is, that plant is *not* safe."

"Of course it is," Royce said, sitting back again at his desk. "No problem about those welds. No need to make a problem. We're talking about stainless steel welds, stronger than the primary material. They've already lasted six years and I wouldn't be surprised they'll last for six thousand years."

"Well, that doesn't leave me with much choice," Godell said. "Somebody ought to take this up with NRC."

Royce's face went ashen. "I wouldn't do that if I were you." He opened a desk drawer and took out a small roll of mints. He popped one in his mouth and then put the roll back. "You'd better think this over very carefully before you start acting on your own initiative. We all know how critical things are just now. This company has all its venture capital on the line and is borrowed to the hilt. A bureaucratic delay could shut this whole op down tight. Think of the loss. And think of the jobs. If I were you—"

"You're not me, Mr. Royce. You're a guy whose nuts could be in the wringer. And I'm sorry for that. On the other hand, I'm sitting over there in that plant and the damn thing is unsafe, not just for me and for all the men who work there, but for Christ knows how many people—"

"Will you slow *down!*" Royce's agitation drew him part way out of his chair. "You're making trouble. Unnecessary trouble. Christ, you ought to know better than to go outside channels. At the very least, take this matter up with whatshisname, Herman De Young, isn't it? Isn't he the overall plant supervisor there? But you can't just ride off on your own and go to the NRC."

Jack stood up. There was nothing more to say. He touched a finger to his forehead in an ironic mock salute and stepped out of the trailer. As he was getting in his car, he saw Royce moving quickly up to another nearby trailer, this one the office of Hugh Redman, the prime contractor for the Point Conception site. As he backed out of his parking slot, Jack saw Royce and another man, Redman perhaps, appear in the doorway, talking together and looking in his direction. He ignored them, and made his way deliberately through the outer gate.

It took him a little better than an hour to get back to his home area and by that time it was too late to go back to the plant. He decided to turn off and head for his apartment. Well, he smiled grimly to himself, De Young had told him to take some time off. He'd taken it off, had put it to good use, but he doubted that De Young would be pleased. As he stepped out of his car in his underground garage, two figures came out of a doorway. Jack was startled and then recognized Kimberly Wells. A young man was with her.

"Mr. Godell, Jack?" Kimberly called.

He didn't answer. He was both embarrassed and irritated by her presence. One thing was certain, he didn't want to talk about those X-rays until he'd had a chance to think things over. And in any case, he wasn't in the habit of airing family laundry in public.

"What now, Miss Wells?" he said, somewhat acidly.

"We'd like to talk to you."

"Some other time, if you don't mind," Jack walked quickly past them and through the garage door. He was just fitting his key in the lock of his apartment when he heard footsteps behind him. As he turned the key and swung the door open, the young man literally shoved him inside.

"What the *hell*—" Jack shouted.

Kimberly closed the door quickly behind them.

"Get out of my apartment. I mean *now*!"

"We won't get out!" Richard shouted back. "You almost killed us!"

"I *what*?" Jack was incredulous. "Hey, this is bananas!" He marched to pick up the telephone, saying over his shoulder to Kimberly, "you get yourself and that creep outta here or he might end in the hospital and both of you in jail."

"You're the one who—" Richard started to roar.

"Richard, shut up! Just *shut up!*" Kimberly's voice was shrill.

Richard regained his composure. Breathing

hard, he pointed a finger at Godell who had paused with the phone in his hand. "O.K., but you can't deny it. We have it all on film."

"What? What are you *talking* about?"

"Jack, please listen," Kimberly entreated. "We had to speak to you. This is my friend, Richard Adams. He's a cameraman. He was with me when we were in the visitor's gallery and he photographed the control room the whole time the accident was going on."

Jack put the phone down. "Did you say he photographed it? Do you know what that means?"

Kimberly ignored the question. "We've just come from the safety hearings up at Point Conception—"

"I showed the film to an engineer there," Richard said, "a nuclear engineer like yourself. He said you almost uncovered the core."

"That's right, Jack," Kimberly said. "So you lied to me. You said it was just a stuck valve."

Jack shook his head. "I can't believe this. Right here in America. I can't believe—hey, I don't have to answer to you, I don't have to talk to you, I don't have to look at you. Now if you don't get out of my apartment right now, I'm gonna call the police and charge you with forcible entry, or whatever, but I'm really gonna charge you. Now do you understand that?"

"O.K., you call the police if you want," Kimberly said resolutely. "But we're staying here until you tell us the truth or we get dragged out." She was astonished at the words coming from her own lips. Whence this impulse? This courage? She knew herself to be a young woman furiously on the make, and suddenly she was Betsy Ross, Barbara Fritchie, Joan of Arc.

And perhaps it was the sight of Kimberly's slightly faltering lower lip, the look of a beautiful young woman with every ounce of her courage screwed into a tiny pressure point, right at the edge of, but not quite reaching, breakdown. Perhaps it was that which reminded him of his own inner struggle and of the need, finally, to lay some of his burden down.

"O.K., O.K.," he said, his voice almost a whisper. "Sit down. You too, Tarzan. Jesus, I hate being pushed around. And in my own—" he rubbed his eyes. They sat down on the edge of overstuffed chairs in his untidy living room and watched, fascinated, as Jack paced up and down a few times without saying anything.

"I am gonna tell you the truth," he said, finally. "I have to. It was—it was much more serious than we let on. The fact is, we almost uncovered the core—"

"That engineer said—" Richard burst.

"Shut up, kid," Jack said, without violence, "let me finish. *Almost* uncovered. But didn't. So there was no accident. There was a chain of—what you could call very dangerous circumstances, but it never got as far as an accident. We took care of it. The system worked. The plant is back on-line. But there's something else—"

"What?" Kimberly was fascinated.

"I want a beer. Anybody want a beer?"

They both shook their heads. Jack went to the fridge, removed a beer and took a long drink before he resumed.

"There's something I—something worse. Goddamnit!" he slapped his hand hard on a table top. The slap was so loud, so surprising that Kimberly jumped. "I love that goddamn plant, you know that?" He wasn't looking at her, he was looking at his framed Navy commission which was hanging over the mantel place. "That plant is my life. Well, anyway, we got her back in business, back on-line. We started her up slow and easy—" He fumbled in a box for a cigarette, lighted it and puffed a long cloud.

"We got up to thirty per cent and there was a small shudder during the trip-out. Just a small shudder. Nobody noticed it but me. And it bothered me. So I checked and we all checked and all we could find was a small leak around the recirculation pump in the containment area. So then we tested the pump and it tested out all right, but damnit, this thing was still gnawing at me.

"So, more to get it off my mind, I went into the records section to check the X-rays of the pump—sure you don't want a beer?"

Kimberly shook her head. Her face was like a mask.

"And I discovered," Jack said tiredly, "that some of the welds on the pump support structures—that is the huge legs that hold that tremendous pump up—some of those welds had not been X-rayed. Somewhere, somehow, some jerk, either lazy, or maybe because they forced him to do it, he just didn't X-ray all the welds. What he did do was reprint X-rays of the same goddamn weld and give them different numbers as if each picture belonged to a different weld. But they didn't. They're all identical. They're all of the same weld." He shrugged. "Look, it happens, right? In other industries? People goof off. Or some officer of the company finds a way to shave a buck and he tells the next man down to cut corners."

"But this isn't just *any* industry," Richard said ominously.

Jack nodded agreement. "Now it doesn't mean those other welds are necessarily substandard, you understand, it just means—"

"It means it isn't safe!" Kimberly said, her voice high with excitement. "Despite all the pious talk about checking and—"

"It means," Godell continued, "the damn thing should be shut down again and all those welds X-rayed again. All those welds in the pump supports, because that's where the leak is, and, I suspect, that's where the shudder may be coming from. And what we're looking at is millions of dollars for radiography, for lost revenue while we're shutdown, maybe public scandal, public inquiries, heads rolling—especially in the construction company whose responsibility it was." He threw his hands in the air.

"One thing more," he added in as soft a

voice as he could manage. "If that pump should rupture or, God forbid, topple, we could be facing a loss-of-coolant type accident."

"Meaning a—a China Syndrome?" Kimberly asked.

Godell looked at her and nodded his head.

"Holy cow!" Richard breathed, a hand to his face, staring at Godell.

"So now that you know what I'm sitting on," Godell said, "maybe you can understand why I get a little upset when you two break into my apartment."

"Sorry about that," Richard said, "but we were concerned too. After all—"

"O.K.," Kimberly said, "I'm a reporter and you can accuse me of wanting to fatten my ass, or make a big name for myself or whatever, but would you consider coming on the news and making this information public? Not with me, necessarily, just—"

Jack shook his head dubiously. "Boy, you're talking to an old Navy man, a company man. We don't go out of the family if we don't have to. Besides, I *like* my job. I've got to remain anonymous."

"I can understand that," Kimberly said. "Still, you agree: something has to be done?"

"Yeah," Jack agreed. He twisted his hands, asking himself what he had done. What had caused this breach of inner discipline? What had driven him to discuss a "family matter" with virtual strangers? Dangerous strangers.

Kimberly noted his unease and felt a pang. She was seeing him in a rare moment of indecision, hesitant, almost naked. She felt both drawn to him and frightened for him. Embarrassed, she turned her gaze away.

"Maybe," Jack said, "we can help each other. Discreetly. I want to get this matter cleared up. But I also have to protect myself. O.K.—if I give you some of these phony X-rays, can you make sure that they're presented as evidence at the Point Conception hearing? Evidence to question the methods of the construction company that has built *both* plants? And can you assure me you'll keep my name out of it? That's vital."

"I know I can," Richard answered quickly. "All I have to do is phone Elliott Lowell and he'll be more than willing to present them."

"And I think I can convince the station," Kimberly said, "to let me take a mobile unit up there to make sure that it all gets on the air—oh, my God!" She looked at her watch. "I'm gonna be late for the six o'clock. Quick, how do we get those X-rays?"

"Tomorrow morning," Godell said. "I'll go to the plant, as usual. Is there someone you can trust who can meet me at the post office about two miles up the road? Say, nine o'clock. It better not be either one of you two, just in case there's a security tail on me. That's possible, you know. See, I already went out on a limb by talking to one of those construction people and they might have the wind up—"

"Hector!" Richard said. "Yeah, we've got someone. Chicano fella, big beefy guy. Nice. Close friend of mine."

"And thank you," Kimberly said, moving to the door. "Really, thank you. I've got to run. But I'll call you." Her pencil was poised.

Jack gave her his phone number and they were out the door. Well, he thought. Well, well. He put down his beer can and went into the kitchen to pour himself a double shot.

At just a few seconds before six o'clock Kimberly and Richard were sprinting down a corridor at the studio. They drew up at a door with a red light shining overhead, DO NOT ENTER WHEN RED LIGHT IS ON. They entered. Mac Churchill, sitting behind the glass screen of the control room, spotted her and moved immediately onto the set.

Just as he did so, the floor manager gave a signal and Pete Martin blazed a smile into the camera. "Good evening, this is Pete Martin. It's six o'clock and time for the news . . ."

Kimberly moved breathlessly into position so that she would be ready to come in on cue, tucking in her blouse, smoothing her hair.

Mac Churchill grabbed her arm and whispered furiously in her ear. "Where the hell have you been? And what's going on? You had a meeting with legal people this afternoon and we waited half an hour for you. Jacovich is having a fit!"

Kimberly kept her eye on Pete Martin, then moved her glance to the floor manager, alert for her cue.

"Where is that goddamn film?" Churchill hissed.

"Better get Jacovich down here," Kimberly

murmured to him. "We have a story like you wouldn't believe!"

Ten seconds, the floor manager signaled silently to Kimberly.

"Hey, listen, girl," Churchill whispered, "I don't care what kind of a story you've got going, you don't order—"

"I said get him down here. And fast," Kimberly said. Then she walked on stage just as Pete Martin cued her: "And now, with California Closeup, here's Kimberly Wells . . ."

Kimberly smiled into the camera and read her lines off the teleprompter. "Thank you, Pete. Tonight on California Closeup we're going to be taking a look at a new kind of doctor—a man who pays house calls to cure—sick fish!"

As the scene changed to show a man in shirt sleeves working over an enameled pan filled with water, and tweezing a stricken guppie out of the pan, Kimberly's voice rode the soundtrack.

"His name is Horace Seward and he lives in Burbank. He says that he decided to specialize in fish medicine after one of his own very expensive fish died when it swallowed the hour hand of a Mickey Mouse wristwatch . . ."

Exactly twenty-eight minutes later, when the news program had signed off, Kimberly, Mac Churchill, Richard Adams and Don Jacovich were closeted in the news conference room.

"I've been wanting to have a little talk with you and your sidekick there," Jacovich said grimly. "Now what's this all about?"

Kimberly quickly outlined the events of the day, recapping the positions of Dr. Elliott Lowell and Greg, the nuclear engineer, and winding up with a resumé of the conversation in Jack Godell's apartment.

"So there you have it. All the facts we've got so far. I know it's not for me to define my role at this station, but I'm tired, Mr. Jacovich. Tired of covering birthday parties for lions at the zoo, tired of talking dogs and sick tropical fish. This is my story, I dug it out, I stayed with it and I'm going to report it live—tomorrow at noon."

"Don't you know who this guy Elliott Lowell is? He's an intervener. A professional troublemaker. Of course he's going to register a beef. That's what certain fringe groups pay him to do!"

"I don't think you understand me. I'm not going to argue this matter," Kimberly said. "Either I report it for this station, and in the way I see fit, or I'm quitting right now and taking my material to another station."

"You wouldn't—"

"Try me."

Jacovich opened his mouth to speak but no words came out. Then he began to close his mouth. It took him a while but he did finally close it. And he looked, Kimberly thought, exactly like a guppie that had swallowed a Mickey Mouse wristwatch. The whole watch.

SEVEN

The following morning Jack was up and out of the shower fast. He flung himself into his BMW, normally the love of his life, and actually abused the car, slamming it into reverse and screeching out of his garage. He wanted to get to the plant just in time for his shift but no later than that. He didn't want there to be any time for phone calls or inter-office memos. Making his way efficiently through security, he bypassed his normal route to his office and went immediately to the records section. Luckily, the place was deserted, the clerk-in-charge out for coffee, or perhaps she hadn't yet arrived. Without difficulty, he located the file he wanted, slipped a stack of X-ray negatives into his briefcase and made his way down the corridor. Just as he reached a tee, he saw Herman De Young and two technicians approaching.

In panic, and wishing he could ditch his briefcase, Jack shrank against a wall and waited. Fortunately, the group made a left turn and passed him by. He waited a few seconds and then walked as quickly as he could without breaking into a run, back the way he'd come.

At the post office, Jack moved up to a table and began taking things out of his briefcase, letters, packages, and the envelope containing the X-rays. Scribbling furiously on the parcel, and pasting stamps on his letters, he almost didn't notice Hector until the burly Chicano "accidentally" nudged his arm. "Sorry," Hector smiled.

"Hector?" Jack muttered under his breath.

Hector nodded and smiled again.

What neither of them noticed at that moment was that a plain blue Chevy had driven up in front of the post office. A man got out on the passenger side, paused in front of the glass door and then entered the post office.

Jack paid him no mind. Instead, he gathered up his letters and parcels, all except the envelope containing the X-rays, and strode off to wait in line. When he glanced back over his shoulder, he saw that Hector had left and so had the envelope of X-rays.

What Jack didn't notice was the man following Hector out. He joined his companion in the blue Chevy, and they swung into traffic on the tail of Hector's little red MG.

By mid-morning the atmosphere at the Point Conception licensing hearings had begun to warm up again. Kimberly arrived, accompanied by Richard and Mac Churchill. Dr. Elliott Lowell approached them and there were introductions all around. For a moment, they listened to a young man who stood in the audience and read from a prepared statement:

"To the Atomic Safety and Licensing Board and to the public at large. I regret that I shall be almost entirely silent today. I would prefer to speak and be heard. But these hearings are not true hearings. They do not exist for the purpose of hearing and weighing public sentiment. Only the voices of the power companies and those of the government are heard and both voices come from the same large body. The NRC has to date held sixty licensing hearings and not once has a license been denied. So these are merely rubber stamp hearings, and we, the public, are too late to have any say in the future of our lives, our children's lives."

Mac gestured to Kimberly and she joined him to walk back out of the hall to their mobile unit. "I hope you've really got something here, kid. It had better be good. Or else."

"It will be," she said calmly, "don't worry."

Back in the hall, another visitor entered. It was MacCormack, chairman of the board of C.G.&E. He sat down next to his public relations man, Bill Gibson, both of them crisply dressed and groomed.

"I see these TV people are back in force," MacCormack said. "Is there any possibility that they might turn over that film to this commission?"

"I don't know," Gibson said, frowning. "I should think they wouldn't. I'd hope they wouldn't—but I honest to God don't know."

Several miles from Point Conception, on the winding Pacific Coast Highway, Hector's little red MG moved with wasplike speed along the ocean's rim. Hector had the top down and the radio up. It was a bright sunny day and he was charged with pleasure and excitement. The X-rays were tucked away in his briefcase on the floor.

Suddenly something moved into his rear view mirror, moving so fast that his breath caught. It was a large, heavy-duty van and it was coming up behind him at a frightening rate.

"The guy must be stoned or out of his mind," Hector thought, uncertain as to whether to slow down and let the guy pass or speed up to avoid a collision. And then he had no more time for making a choice.

The van slammed into his rear end. Hector screamed and instinctively jammed his brakes. But the forward speed and mass of the van was too great. The little MG bucked and shrieked, tires smoking, glass splintering, fuel spewing out onto the highway. Hector fought the wheel to stay on the road. Then he lost it. "Son of a—" he screamed. But the scream was lost when the little red car hit the guard rails, leaped, crashed and rolled down the embankment.

The van pulled up at the side of the road and a man got out. He walked slowly, deliberately, across the open highway and stared down at the embankment. The MG was utterly demolished and silent, except for one wheel spinning slowly to a stop.

In the high school gymnasium at Point Conception, Kimberly checked her watch nervously. Dr. Elliott Lowell was scheduled to begin his testimony soon and he too was checking his watch and then turning in his seat to search the rear of the gymnasium. Then he turned back and flashed a glance of hopelessness to Richard. Richard came up to Kimberly and whispered in her ear. She nodded and then slipped out of the gym into the corridor.

A few moments later the telephone rang in Jack Godell's apartment. He picked up the phone and listened, cautiously.

"Jack," Kimberly said, "did you make the transfer? As we agreed last night."

"Yeah, kid," Jack said. "About—" he looked at his watch, "hour and a half, two hours ago. He shouldda—"

"Well, he hasn't." She paused. "Jack, Lowell is about to go on and we have nothing. He's going to look foolish and I'm going to—well, we'll be destroyed, that's all. You've got to come over and help us."

"No!" Jack said. His reply was immediate and instinctive.

"It's not just us, Jack, it's for everybody. You've got to come and testify. We must use your name. You must tell them what you told us last night."

"I can't."

"But—"

"I can't," Jack said, feeling panic rise. "It's out of the question. People like me just don't—I'm sorry. I've done what I could." Then, before she could say anything more, he put down the phone.

Kimberly put the phone back on the hook and said tiredly to Richard, "No dice. He gave it to Hector about an hour and a half, two hours ago. And he won't come down, won't say a word." She shrugged. "We've had it."

Back in his flat, Godell moved uneasily from the kitchen to the front of his apartment, feeling an urge to take a drink and fighting it down. His agitation was great, but on one point he was very clear. He would not, repeat, not show up at the licensing hearing and put everything he'd worked for on the line. It suddenly occurred to him that he wanted to be out of his apartment in case the phone rang again. He peered through a curtain before leaving and then he saw something that gave him a shock. Two men in a plain blue Chevy were sitting across the street from his apartment. Cautiously, so as not to move the curtains, he withdrew. There was no question about it: they had a tail on him, possibly had one on him ever since he left the plant at Point Conception. Had they bugged his apartment, his phone? He quickly unscrewed the mouthpiece of the telephone and found no telltale disc. Still, they could have bugged it in a dozen other ways. Feeling the sweat break out on the back of his neck, he let himself out of the apartment and tiptoed out to the garage.

Standing beside his car, he hesitated. Then, doubting that they would pull anything inside a garage, he unlocked the car and started the engine. Turning briskly out into the street, he made a quick right turn, instead of going along the avenue for half a mile as he usually did. Sure enough, a few seconds later, he spotted the blue Chevy in the glass.

The scene in the high school gymnasium was getting increasingly taut. Two large, uniformed, gun-packing U.S. marshals had moved into position beside Bill Gibson, obviously waiting for his order to confiscate the film in the event that it was shown. Dr. Elliott Lowell had just moved into position before the Licensing Commission and was doing a very unconvincing job of shuffling papers, stalling for time.

Kimberly spoke in an urgent undertone to one of her colleagues at the camera van. "Red, call the station for me right away. Have them check police reports for any accidents along the coast highway in the last couple of hours. We're looking for a little red MG."

"Dr. Elliott," the chairman of the commission cleared his throat. "It's now eleven-fifteen. Do you think you could get started?"

"Mr. Chairman," Lowell said, "there has been some delay in getting the evidence that I intend to present to this hearing. I should like to request a postponement of my appearance until tomorrow. At the same time."

This was greeted with a low moan of disappointed murmurs from the audience. Many of them were counting on Dr. Lowell, and they had sensed he was going to make an important disclosure.

"Dr. Elliott," the chairman said, trying to mask impatience, "if you're not prepared to present your testimony at this time, I think I must ask you to yield."

Kimberly's intercom beeped and she picked

up the transceiver and listened, nodded, then hastened to Richard's side. "There's been an accident about ten miles back along the highway," she said. "Red MG. Totaled."

Richard was out of his chair at once and racing for his jeep, Kimberly running a few paces behind.

Lowell had nothing more to say and was obliged to step down. The Chairman called a recess. The crowd of protesters wilted in their chairs.

Only Bill Gibson was discreetly jubilant. He told a small assembly of newspeople, "You've just seen another example of the sort of thing the utility companies have learned to live with. Scare tactics, delays, irresponsible protests. A small group of people, I won't call them paranoid, but they do see large corporations as uniformly wicked, diabolical. These people are causing the utility companies costly delays. I mean very costly. We have to pay dearly for these delays and ultimately, those costs have to be paid by the consumer, by you and me."

While Kimberly and Richard were racing to the scene of Hector's accident, Jack Godell was having traffic problems of his own. Stopped at a red light, he could see the blue Chevy a couple of cars behind him. A car with three teenagers and a large dog pulled up alongside him. Anxiously glancing in their direction, Jack received a smiling gesture from one of the teenagers, "the Finger." The dog barked loudly and ferociously. The light was just about to change when an ambulance came screaming along the cross street and Jack had to jam his clutch back again to keep from leaping forward. Then, instinctively, before anybody else had a chance to recover, he jumped across the intersection before the light turned green and made a wheel-smoking getaway.

Barreling up the freeway ramp and calmer now that he had lost his tail, he switched his radio on and fiddled with the dial. Emerging onto the freeway at high speed, he caught the end of a live broadcast from Point Conception. What he heard wasn't much, but it was enough. Dr. Elliott Lowell, interviewed by a radio reporter, said that he had had to postpone his testimony because the evidence he needed hadn't arrived in time. The man who was carrying that evidence was reported to have had a serious accident on the coast highway. Authorities were checking now.

Jesus! Jack said, half-aloud. They're really out for blood. And no sooner had he had that thought, than he was aware that the blue Chevy was not only on his tail but overtaking him in the outside lane. He floor-boarded the BMW and felt the powerful engine buck into high. Veering ahead and into the extreme left lane, Godell out-accelerated the Chevy, picked up a few hundred precious yards, and then he made a sharp, go-for-broke turn across traffic, slewing and screaming toward an off-ramp. The little car weaved and skidded but held. As he raced down the ramp, he got a last glimpse of the Chevy, skidding badly and narrowly missing the guard rail, but headed for the ramp behind him.

Still, he had gained a few hundred yards and would gain a bit more when he turned off the ramp and headed under the underpass. Once more he down-shifted into a racing turn, skidding the little car expertly, blessing the tough, high-performance suspension of the BMW. Still turning high rpm's as he came into the plant entrance, he drew up to a screeching stop at the gate.

"Jesus, Mr. Godell," the guard said, holstering his revolver. "You coulda got yourself shot coming up here like that."

"Sorry, Mike, but it's urgent. Let me through, will you?"

"Sure." The bar swung up, Jack dashed across the lot to his assigned parking space and got out of the car. Behind him, he could see that the blue Chevy had parked alongside the chain-link fence on the peripheral road to the plant. But they hadn't come onto the entrance way. He trotted across the lot in the direction of his office.

At the accident site along the coast highway, a crew of rescue workers were preparing to put Hector on a stretcher.

He flickered back and forth between consciousness and coma, pressure bandages on his face and hands and scalp. Fortunately, he'd been thrown clear when the car rolled.

Richard sprinted down the embankment to Hector's side and reached him just as the rescuers had him on a basket litter. An ambulance stood flashing patiently at the shoulder of the highway.

"Heck! It's Richard. Can you hear me?"

Kimberly tottered down. "Is he alive?" she asked a young doctor. He nodded.

"Hey!" a policeman called to Richard, "leave him alone. Get outta there."

Richard ignored him. "Hector, where are those X-rays? Heck, this is Richard. Look at me."

"He's going out," the doctor said. "I had to give him a shot."

Suddenly, Hector's eyes opened, wide but unfocused. He tried to speak but no words came.

"Officer," Kimberly said, when the policeman strode angrily over. "We're close friends. Were you the first one here?"

The cop softened his stance when he saw her concern. "Yes, ma'am. I should think I got here within minutes. The car was totaled. I phoned it in."

"He was carrying some important papers," Kimberly said. "Has anybody touched anything, taken anything out of his car?"

"Don't see how," the cop said. "The car was almost totally destroyed. See for yourself."

Steeling herself, Kimberly moved to the MG. It was true that the car had been almost totally destroyed but the interior was only partially wrecked. The front seat area had not been completely destroyed. In fact she could discern fresh blood, darker than the red vinyl upholstery.

"Nothing," Richard said, having moved up behind her. "No trace of those negs."

Kimberly turned to look at him. His face had no expression but in his eyes there was a look that she had seen before. It seemed to say clearly: I told you it would be like this.

Jack Godell buzzed the control room door. The guard inside checked his TV monitor, recognized Godell, checked his ID and admitted him. Jack nodded to the other control personnel and moved quickly into his office. As he touched his desk he had a shock of recognition. He could feel the turbines vibrating far below. "Hey, Ted—"

Spindler appeared in his doorway.

"What's going on? Feels like the power is up—"

"Yeah, right. De Young's orders. We'll be up to full by midnight."

"We'll be up—we can't. We've got to shut down, Ted."

Spindler stared at him, uncomprehending.

"Listen Ted, I found out that the support structures on the recirc pump could be defective. Remember that leak? And those shudders? Well, I discovered that a whole bunch of those Quality Assurance reports were faked. So any sudden surge, a SCRAM, anything, might kick off a vibration."

Spindler blinked, trying to digest this information. A part of him was beginning to wonder if Jack were drunk or possibly, deranged.

"Wh—what are you—shut down?"

"Got to," Jack insisted. "We've had enough danger signs, and there's enough cause for doubt."

"Hey, Jack." Spindler held up his hands almost as if he were fending Godell off, fending something off. "I'm not shutting down. O.K.? My orders are to start up. That's what I've done." Not trusting himself to say any more, Spindler turned on his heel and moved to his console.

Jack hesitated a moment and then walked out into the control room. He glanced around at the various indicators, nodded abstractedly to the technicians and then moved forward to talk to Spindler again. Spindler, however, saw him coming and moved across the room to talk to another aide.

A technician called out: "We're at seventy-five per cent of full power. Recirc flow at eighty per cent normal. Zenon operation is normal."

"Okay," Spindler said, looking up from a print-out sheet, "keep her moving. Let's take it up to ninety-three per cent with the recirc."

As he said this, he darted a glance at Godell. Godell stood looking at the indicator panels for a moment, blocked and frustrated, then he moved to the guard's desk.

"Fred," he told the uniformed guard, "let me out, will you?"

Fred nodded and swiveled slightly in his chair to punch a control button on the door. Jack swooped quickly and snatched the pistol from his holster.

"Hey—"

Everyone turned. What they saw was Jack Godell, their boss, the calm and seasoned veteran, now standing in the control room, his body gripped with unmistakable tension, and in his hands a huge, menacing gun.

"Out!" Jack shouted, his voice high but clear, "Everybody. I said out of this room. I mean it!"

They were paralyzed for a moment.

Spindler stepped forward. "Jack, for Christ's sake. Don't do this—"

Godell turned and pointed the pistol at Spindler, thumbing the hammer back.

"Ted, so help me," Jack said ominously. Then he raised his voice again. "I said out and I mean out. Go on, Ted."

Spindler shrugged and moved to the door. In a few minutes, the other technicians, not quite able to believe that they were closeted with a madman, but not quite able *not* to believe it, had filed out the door. Jack was now totally alone in the locked control room. He was solely in charge of the entire plant. Up in the visitor's gallery, jittery technicians were gathering to watch him. And they were being joined by others as the news spread through the plant.

A helicopter set down just as Hector's body was being loaded into the ambulance. Bill Gibson jumped out and trotted quickly to where Richard Adams and Kimberly were watching.

"What'd you do, come back to make sure he was finished?" Adams said snarling. "You gonna kick him in the head?"

"Now look, I had nothing to do with this accident—"

"Accident!" Kimberly's voice broke. "That was no accident and you—"

"Damnit, listen to me," Gibson implored. "Jack Godell has taken over the control room of the Ventana plant. He's got a gun. I think he's gone crazy. He's alone in there and nobody can get in. He wants to talk to you."

Kimberly stared at Richard. He looked back at her, bewildered.

"I'm begging you, Miss Wells—" There was a quality in Gibson's tone that was surprisingly human. "If he's cracked up, alone in there, in command of that entire reactor . . . Please! He asked for you—"

A few moments later they were all in the helicopter as it lifted above the scene of the accident.

EIGHT

The entire Ventana power plant was in a state of crackling urgency. Engineers were poring over blueprints, trying to determine a method of blocking the controls from the central control room, trying to find a means of neutralizing that control center and looking for a loophole in a system that had been ingeniously devised to prevent just such a seizure from the outside.

In the turbine building, men wearing radiation suits and carrying oxygen packs lounged on standby, smoking and sweating inside their heavy suits as they waited for God-knows what kind of emergency. Elsewhere, technicians and engineers were examining electrical relays and referring back to drawings in the vain hope that there was some way they might block signals coming from that vital center where Jack Godell reigned supreme.

At that moment, Bill Gibson, accompanied by Kimberly and Richard, strode into the visitor's gallery. De Young was there and also MacCormack, crusty but authoritative, ever the chairman of the board.

They entered just in time to hear Godell's

voice over the intercom. He sounded harassed but in command of himself.

"Look," he said, "I know what you're trying to do and you'd better knock it off. I can tell somebody is trying to tamper with the security circuits. Tell them to cut it out, right now. If I open one of those large relief valves when we're running like this, it's gonna cost this company lotsa bucks. Do you read me out there?"

De Young shuddered and refrained from looking at his chief. MacCormack's voice was even and entirely without emotion. "He's talking sense," the chairman said. "Better quit that fiddling."

De Young nodded and moved to an intercom. "Ted Spindler," he called and received an acknowledgment. "He's on to you guys. Better knock it off."

Spindler's voice crackled back. "For God's sake, unless we can get into containment to block those security circuits—"

"Find another way," De Young's voice was curt. "You've got to get into that control room."

Then, seeing Kimberly, he switched his intercom button to another position.

"Jack," he called, "Herman De Young. Do you read me?"

"Loud and clear, Herman."

"I've got Kimberly Wells here now."

There was a pause. Then, "Bring her down. Just Kimberly Wells, you understand. Nobody else."

Kimberly stared down at Jack Godell and

saw that he was peering up at her. But because he was shielding his eyes against the bright light of the control room, she could not see the expression in his eyes. She had no way of judging whether or not he had gone completely insane. And what's more, she realized suddenly, she had no choice. She had to go to him.

She nodded to De Young.

"We'll be right down. I'll guide her to the door and then withdraw back around the corridor. You'll be able to see it all on your monitor. There won't be any tricks," De Young said.

Then, to Kimberly, he said, "O.K.?"

She didn't answer and she didn't look at anybody until the door had closed behind her.

Without another word, De Young took her down a flight of stairs, accompanied her to the end of a short corridor and motioned. "Just beyond there. You O.K.?"

Kimberly said nothing. She was too frightened. She walked the last few yards alone, turned a corner and found herself facing a heavy door with a thick bullet-proof panel in it. A small TV camera swept her as she stood.

She was startled by a sudden voice rasping out of an intercom beside her. "Press the button beside the door," Jack said. "Then I'll open it and you walk straight through."

The door slid open, revealing another door identical to the outer door. The outer door slid closed behind her, the inner door opened, and she saw Jack, crouched behind a desk with a pistol trained at her head.

When the door had closed and locked behind her, he got up slowly, lowered the pistol and said, "Welcome to beautiful downtown Ventana." It was a feeble joke and his voice cracked, but she was grateful. Almost hysterically grateful. He was not, thank God, crazy.

"Coffee?" he asked, still shaky, but trying to make her feel comfortable.

She shook her head.

"What happened to the kid, the boy who picked up those negs from me?"

"Accident," Kimberly said. "We're not sure how. Rammed from behind, it looked like. Car destroyed but he's still alive. Or was. Badly hurt—"

"Accident!" Jack snorted. "That was no accident. A couple of them tried to get me too."

"The X-rays were gone. Somebody took them before the cops got there."

Godell paced back and forth, rubbing his chin with a clenched fist. "Goddamn them," he intoned, "goddamn them. I *want* to talk now. I really want to tell the public what happened. Do you understand? I've had it. I'm going to go on television—live. I want you to interview me."

Kimberly nodded. She understood fully what he was saying. Yet all of this was coming through to her as if it were somehow muffled. As if a thick quilt buffered impulses between her sensors and her brain. She looked up and saw that all the people in the visitor's gallery were peering anxiously down at them.

In one corner of the gallery, Gibson had taken Richard Adams aside and was pleading with him in a low, but urgent, voice. "You've got to talk him out of that, Richard," he said. "For his own safety, if for no other reason. We've managed to keep this thing in the family so far. But you've got to try to get him out of there or soon it will be in police hands. They'll have a SWAT team in here—"

MacCormack intervened. "Get him to come out," he urged, "and we'll let him speak his peace. We'll give him whatever hearing he wants. But get him to come out before someone gets hurt."

Richard shook his head. "You guys still don't understand. You never do. You keep on bargaining as if you held all the cards. If I were you, I'd let him do his TV interview or else he'll flood the containment with radiation—like he threatens."

"I don't think—can he do that?" MacCormack asked De Young.

De Young nodded and sighed. "It's just a matter of opening those large relief valves. Right now he can do just about anything he wants. And he knows this plant like the back of his hand. If he floods the containment, we might as well close it all down and bury it."

MacCormack turned back to Richard. "Whatever he wants, he's got. You tell him that. On the air—whatever. We give in."

Gibson shouted. "But that's insane! You can't let him go on TV!"

"Shut up!" MacCormack snapped. "Guard," he called, "keep an eye on this fellow for a bit. Let him make his call. We'll be back in a minute."

Richard spoke into the intercom. "Jack? Kimberly? Listen, this is Richard. They've agreed. Completely. I'm gonna call the station. Not just our station, every damn station in L.A. They can put their cameras up here, they can pick up your voice over the intercom. Is that O.K. with you down there?"

Richard peered down. He could not see Godell because he had withdrawn under the overhang of the visitor's gallery. But he could see Kimberly. She looked first at Godell, and then, having evidently received his approval, nodded a distinct "yes."

Outside in the corridor, MacCormack, De Young and Gibson were in a quick strategy session. "I must say, as your public relations counselor," Gibson said, "this will be ruinous. I can't think of a worse way to—"

"What's your alternative?" MacCormack snapped. "Lose your image or lose a billion-dollar investment? We've just bought ourselves some time. It'll take at least an hour, maybe more to get a full crew of TV and press people here. And maybe we can stall that somehow. The more time we have—"

"It won't take them an hour, not when they hear—"

"O.K. you take care of the press. That's what you're paid for."

"In that case," Gibson said, flushing, "I'd better get ready for them. If you'll excuse me—" He made his exit.

MacCormack now turned on De Young. His tiger mask was back in place and his fangs were bared. "Now what's holding you people up?"

De Young shook his head. "Mr. MacCormack, you've spent a fortune on security in this place. Everything is designed to prevent a forced entry, a take-over of that control room."

"Don't you think I know that?" MacCormack snarled. "Listen, De Young, I'm getting tired of hearing what you can't do. I want to know what you *can* do."

"De Young hesitated. "Well, the only other choice, as I see it—we'll have to try to SCRAM the plant. If we can get it on automatic, we take it out of his hands and then—"

"How're you going to do it?"

"Emergency shutdown," De Young said quickly. "There's some risk, but—a quick insertion of the control rods into the reactor core. If that process can be initially triggered without Godell knowing, then we're on automatic. There's very little he can do at that point to prevent SCRAM. But he'll try. He'll try every possible way. And that might just give us enough time to break in there."

MacCormack drummed his fingers, thinking. "You think you can do that without that maniac catching on?"

"I think we've got to try."

"O.K., then do it!" MacCormack snapped. "SCRAM the son of a bitch. Just let me know when you're ready."

"Yes, sir," De Young said. He moved quickly down the hall.

MacCormack watched him retreating, then turned and went back inside the visitor's gallery. He could see Kimberly sitting next to

Godell who was at the center console, sweeping his eyes continually across the illuminated panel, one hand still holding the gun. Suddenly, he turned to look at her and a faint smile appeared on his face. She smiled in return and reached across and took his open hand.

Elsewhere in the plant, De Young stood anxiously watching a crew of technicians under the guidance of Ted Spindler. They had removed the doors from several large electrical relay panels and were testing circuits with their probes. Spindler brought a blueprint over to De Young for his perusal.

"So we'd need to get on the outside of the containment interlock to SCRAM the reactor directly?" De Young's mouth felt dry. It had been a long time since he'd had anything to eat or drink. His shoulders felt sore after hours of tension.

Barney, one of the technicians in the control room, responded to his question. "That's right, Mr. De Young, but there's one thing here I'm thinking about." He pointed a finger at a position on the blueprint. "By getting control over the generator circuits we could cause a generator and turbine trip. That would eventually cause the reactor to SCRAM."

Spindler rubbed his cheek and moved his bulk uneasily. "Herman," he said, "you realize this is exactly what Godell's so spooked about? A SCRAM at full power?"

"Whose side you on, Ted?" De Young said. "Maybe you want to go up there and give him a hand?"

"Hey, I was just—" Spindler threw up his hands and went back to supervise the technicians.

"How long will it take you?" De Young snapped at Barney. "We'll have to bridge around a dozen circuits, but most of them terminate here, one way or the other. Could take thirty minutes, as much as an hour. Hard to say yet."

It was night now, and the Ventana plant was an island of white light in a sea of semidesert darkness. And coming down into that sea of light was a continuing drone of helicopters, blades stuttering, lights flashing. On the peripheral road there was a stream of vehicles, many of them with dome flashers—police, fire, as well as the many news media vehicles. Richard Adams got out of the KITV mobile unit and had his camera ready just outside the turbine building. Nearby, Bill Gibson was already being interviewed by a TV newsman.

"What's happening inside," Gibson said gravely, "is that an employee, a man who was about to be discharged as a result of this week's incident, has barricaded himself inside the plant. Please be assured that there is no danger to the public whatsoever. Moreover, we should have the situation under control any moment now."

"Tell me a little about this employee, Mr. Gibson," the reporter asked. "Is he, in your judgment a fully sane man?"

"I'm not qualified to answer that," Gibson said. "Naturally that's a medical decision. I can say that he is obviously quite disturbed. We understand there may have been some family problems . . . some alcoholism."

"We understand one of his demands is to make a public statement on television."

"Yes," Gibson said, "I've heard that too. But we're negotiating with him now and we don't think that will be necessary."

The influx of news people and their vehicles, police and fire vehicles and other pieces of equipment, was transforming the normally placid Ventana plant into something that looked like a major disaster site. Gibson excused himself and trotted off to greet a newly arrived news team.

Inside the plant, where De Young was conferring with his aides, a fully equipped SWAT team, in their helmets, flak vests and assault rifles, were quietly going over their procedures. Their commander, a middle-aged veteran said, "According to the plant manager, none of us knows what condition this guy is in. But if you see his hands move to a control, that's it. Waste him."

A few feet away, Richard Adams and his camera crew began to set up their equipment.

"How we going to work this?" one cameraman asked Richard.

"Just like I did before," Richard answered. "We'll shoot through the glass and get our audio over the intercom."

Outside, in the KXLA van, Mac Churchill was sitting before a bank of monitors, talking into a hand mike.

"This is Churchill," he said. "Tell them,

whenever we have to, we'll interrupt regular programming and we'll be coming in fast. Has he put on the standby spots yet? Good. It looks like we're getting close."

Suddenly, Bill Gibson's head appeared in the van doorway. "Hey, Mac," he protested, "this is totally irresponsible."

Churchill hugged his earphones. "Can't hear you, Gibson. Can't hear you." It had been a long time since Churchill had gone out to cover a big story live and his adrenalin was pumping the way it used to.

In the control room itself, Kimberly, still holding Jack Godell's hand, looked up at the visitor's gallery and tried to make out Richard through the shining glass.

"Kimberly—" It was Richard on the intercom. "We'll talk directly into the intercom. Keep the key open all the time. If you two would move just a little closer, it'll give me a better shot. Fine, like that. We're almost there now, 'bout to get this show on the road."

Kimberly looked at Godell. His face was pale and not smiling now.

Up in the visitor's gallery, MacCormack watched helplessly and angrily as the cameras were moved into position.

A cameraman signaled to Richard. "We're just about hooked up, Richard."

Richard signaled jubilantly through the glass and then spoke into the intercom. "Almost there—hang on, kids. You're about to make history."

"Standing by," Kimberly answered.

MacCormack, unable to stand it any longer,

grabbed a phone at his elbow and growled. "De Young? Goddamnit, *do* something. That son of a bitch is about to go on the air."

Down in the cable spreading room, Spindler, aware of De Young's urgency, communicated a sense of emergency to his crew. He was tormented. As much as there was a need for haste, there was a need for caution and precision as well.

"Marty," Spindler spoke into his walkie-talkie, "you're going to have to short that circuit exactly on my signal. If you're one second too soon, it'll tip him off to the whole thing. Got that?" He turned to a nearby technician.

"Marty's down there and ready, standing by. Let us know the moment you're all set."

Frantically, like desperate but skillful surgeons, the men continued their delicate cutting and changing of multi-colored wires.

In the control room, Jack Godell licked his lips and fussed with his tie. "What do I do? I've got whatdoyoucallit. Stage fright. You'll have to tell me when to start, how slow, how fast—"

"When the red light comes on over that camera up there," Kimberly said, "we'll be on the air. All you do is start talking. I don't know, 'Ladies and gentlemen, my name is Jack Godell, I'm locked in the control room of Ventana and I want to explain why.' Don't worry. I'll help you with questions if I think you're getting stuck or if you're not clear."

Back at the KXLA studio, Pete Martin awaited his cue to begin his nightly broadcast. As he did so, he added a short prepared statement: "We interrupt our regular programming to bring you exclusive and live coverage from the Ventana Nuclear Power Plant were an employee has taken over the control center at the plant and is demanding to be heard on TV. Our live camera is there and our own Kimberly Wells is with that man inside the control room . . ."

In the control room, Kimberly, getting all of this through her head set, watched for a signal from the visitor's gallery above. She saw the red light go on, then Richard's finger pointing to her. She touched Jack's sleeve to indicate that he was to hold, and she began, ad lib:

"This is Kimberly Wells. I'm here in the control room at Ventana Nuclear Power Plant with Mr. Jack Godell who has, by using a pistol, taken over the control of this plant. Mr. Godell has resisted all of management's requests to come out of the control room until he has been able to make his statement on TV. Mr. Godell, it's all yours—"

She turned to Jack and indicated he was to begin speaking.

"I—uh—I'm Jack Godell," Jack said, his voice almost cracking at first, but gathering strength. "I'm a shift supervisor here at the Ventana Plant—that is, I'm normally in charge of everything that happens in this room. So I want you to know that I'm not going to hurt anybody and I'm not going to destroy all of southern California. I mean, I'm a trained nuclear engineer. This is my profession. And I'm not crazy either—no matter what the management thinks." He flashed a quick smile at Kimberly and received an encouraging smile in return.

"O.K.—I've been working here for many years. Last Monday at about three-thirty in the afternoon, we had an event here . . ."

Upstairs, Richard looked down at Kimberly and caught her eye. He was feeling tremendous. He lifted his arms and clasped his hands above his head in a gesture of triumph.

Godell's voice continued, loud and clear. "We had a near-accident. The result of human error due to a water level indicator that wasn't working well. The needle stuck. No one was hurt, that's true. But the thing was more serious than the public was led to believe . . ."

In the cable spreading room, Spindler reached into a relay box and hooked a last alligator clip to a terminal. Instantly, his hand flashed up in a signal. In one corner, a man spoke into a walkie-talkie.

Out in the corridor, where he was waiting with the commander of the SWAT team and his men, De Young's walkie-talkie erupted. "De Young, this is Robertson. It's done. We've got it!"

Back in the visitor's gallery, they listened to Godell's voice on the intercom. "As a result of this stuck needle, we began trying to keep additional feedwater from entering the system . . ."

Richard groaned, talking to himself. "Don't get so technical," he muttered. "They won't understand you . . ."

The phone buzzed. MacCormack snatched at it. "We're ready," De Young said, "ready to trip the generator, ready to begin SCRAM procedure. I want your explicit authorization."

"For Christ's sake, *do* it!" MacCormack shouted.

Down in the control room, Kimberly was standing close to Godell, her hand not quite touching his shoulder.

"In actuality," Godell was saying, "the reactor vessel water was critically low. With the main steam line isolated; we only had one auxiliary feedwater pump to get more water into the core. In addition, the water pressure was still above 400 psi, thus the L.P.C.I. wouldn't be activated. But it wasn't the accident that got me into this place, it was something else. I'm not making much sense, I know, but—" He glanced at Kimberly and she smiled and indicated that he should continue.

Suddenly some annunciators on the generator console began to beep. Jack spun around and looked at the monitors. The annunciators on the turbine console began to sound. He moved over to that panel.

Alarmed, Kimberly followed him. "Jack—" she called.

He was about to turn and speak when all hell broke loose. Lights began flashing, alarms sounded, a loud klaxon began to bray. There was no mistaking it, a SCRAM condition was under way.

"Oh, no—" Jack gasped. He yelled something to Kimberly but she could not hear him over the volume of hysterical noise.

Out in the corridor, Herman De Young, holding a fire axe, stood back as members of the

SWAT team methodically tamped plastic explosive around the edges of the heavy control room door. Suddenly, spying a heavy TV cable across the end of the corridor, De Young moved quickly, swinging his axe and cutting the cable in two.

Immediately, the red light on the camera went off. "We're not getting any picture!" the cameraman yelled to Richard.

Back at KXLA control room, the monitor went black. Pete Martin went on the air. "Stand by please, we've temporarily lost our picture due to technical reasons, but—"

Inside the control room, Jack Godell was frantically trying to manipulate controls. He shouted above the racket. "My God! This is the very thing I was trying to prevent. Those idiots! Suicidal idiots!"

Richard's voice came over the intercom. "We're off the air, Kimberly. Those bastards cut the cable."

"Damn!" Kimberly said, crying. "Damn them! Damn—"

There was a loud explosion and a concussive movement of air in the control room as the heavy door was blown off its hinges. The SWAT team poured in.

"Jack!" Kimberly screamed.

He didn't hear. His attention was fixed on the console, desperately trying to correct what he knew would be a disastrous situation.

Godell moved to the TV monitor stationed at the recirculation pump and peered at it, praying that the pump would hold under this sudden surge of pressure.

The SWAT commander entered, leveling his gun at Godell.

"Freeze!" he yelled.

Godell couldn't or wouldn't hear.

"No!" Kimberly screamed.

The policeman fired. Godell spun and fell to the floor.

Kimberly reached him just as De Young and Spindler and other technicians came pouring in behind the SWAT team.

Spindler took a quick look at the annunciators and then stopped, stared at Jack. He was suddenly appalled by the sight of blood.

"My God," he gasped. "Jack—"

Kimberly, her head close to Godell, was trying to stop the flow of blood. He lay with his cheek to the floor, his lips moving.

"I can hear it," he whispered. "I can hear it."

"What?" Spindler asked.

"He said 'I can hear it.' What?" Kimberly said.

And then they all heard it. And felt it. It was an immense and unnatural vibration from somewhere deep in the bowels of the plant. Spindler's face blanched. He leaped to the TV monitor of the pump. And he could see only a portion of what the monitor saw.

Down in that dread cavern, the huge pump was beginning to quiver and twist on its mounts as the tremendous torsion of the impeller moved huge volumes of water. Alarm systems were being triggered one by one. The entire system, hundreds of tons in weight and several stories high began to jiggle and move as if it were a child's toy. A crack began to open at the edge of one weld.

Suddenly, one pump support started to buckle, pieces of stainless steel splintering and flying through the cave like shell fragments. Electric cables, sheared by this flying steel, erupted into clusters of blue and orange sparks.

In the control room, the tableau had gone silent. Godell's head lay on Kimberly's knee, Richard beside her. The man was clearly dying. Spindler was frozen with terror and indecision before the TV monitor.

The lights went off and the room was plunged in darkness. There were shouts. The light went on again as the emergency lighting system took over.

Spindler looked away from the monitor, unconsciously waiting for Godell to take over the problem and solve it. But he could see that Godell was dead.

In the cavern housing the pump, the massive supports were completely gone. The immense pump was held only by a web of its own piping, tilted, dancing, skittering, swaying up and down—but holding. Then, suddenly, the engine sounds fell away. The pump stopped its whine. It gave a final shudder and then all motion stopped.

In the control room, Spindler, hands shaking, pulled out a computer print-out sheet. He read:

CORE TEMP 502
502
499

RHR NORM
STABLE SHUTDOWN
STABLE SHUTDOWN
EVENT ENDS 2332:05 P

EVENT DURATION 3:00:25

"It's over," Spindler said to Kimberly. "It's—it's O.K. now."

Kimberly nodded and then she turned to Richard. "Did any of that—I mean, how much of it got on the air?"

"Enough," Richard said bitterly. "Just enough to make Godell look like a lunatic."

A little later, outside the power plant, Bill Gibson was fielding questions and answers at an impromptu press conference.

"Hold on—one question at a time—yes, you there—Mr. Godell was shot. That's right, by the SWAT team. I'm not sure who fired the actual shot. Yes, I'm told he's dead."

"Do we understand," a reporter asked, "that Godell had been fired? Or was about to be? What did Godell do at the plant? What did he have to do with the accident?"

"Gentlemen, I'll answer all those questions in a release, if you'll just let me get to my office." He glanced at Kimberly and Richard as they moved past this body of news people. "I just want to stress," Gibson continued, "that at no time was the public in any danger. The disturbed employee was humored just long enough so that we could get the situation in hand."

Richard took Kimberly's arm. "The same

old shit," he snarled, "just like grandmaw used to make."

Kimberly hung back. She wanted to hear Gibson.

"Unfortunately," Gibson said, "Mr. Godell did do some damage to the plant, but that damage was completely contained—" He broke off as he saw MacCormack coming forward, accompanied by Herman De Young and Ted Spindler.

"Gentlemen—" Gibson called out, "I'd like you to meet Mr. Ted Spindler, the man who was in charge of the accident throughout and who devised the procedure for preventing any major damage. Mr. Spindler has been with the company for many years, since even before it went into nuclear power."

Reporters immediately clustered around Spindler and began thrusting microphones at him.

"How long did you know Godell . . . ?"

"How'd you stop him . . . ?"

"Were you scared?"

"Was there a near-disaster?"

"I—I—" Spindler faltered.

"Give him a chance to tell his story," Gibson suggested.

"How'd you stop him? Was Godell trying to blow up the joint?"

"We—uh—crossed some circuits in the cable spreading room," Spindler said. "And then we SCRAMMED the plant."

Kimberly grabbed the microphone from a KXLA reporter. "Let me have it, O.K.?"

Kimberly pushed and shoved her way

through the mass of reporters. They were like hungry sharks around a piece of fresh meat. Panting from exertion, she finally reached the front row and shoved her microphone in Spindler's face.

"Mr. Spindler," she exhorted, "Mr. Spindler. Is it true that Jack Godell was disturbed?"

Her question could scarcely be heard in the din of other questions. "Is it true that Jack Godell was disturbed?" she repeated, raising her voice.

"Will you let me ask a question!" She shouted it angrily.

She got Spindler's attention at last. "I'm asking you: was Jack Godell disturbed? You knew him well, didn't you?"

Spindler stared at her and then stared at Bill Gibson.

"I'll ask you again: is it true that Jack Godell was, as they say, disturbed?"

"Well, he was—I—"

Spindler wanted to evade this angry young woman.

"*Was* he?" Kimberly persisted. "Disturbed?"

"Uh, no. No, he wasn't."

A sudden hush fell over the reporters in the crowd. They fell back slightly to give Kimberly more room.

"Mr. Gibson just told us that Godell had been drinking. To your knowledge, was that true?"

"Oh, well, drinking," Spindler said. "He might have had a couple. You know—we all did. Every night, we'd meet at this bar we go to and we'd have a couple. But Jack wasn't what you'd call a big drinker. I mean I've known him for years. He's been at half a dozen parties at my house."

"So he was in no sense an habitual drunk."

"Good God, no," Spindler said.

"Then how do *you* explain his behavior tonight? I know you saw him. What did he say to you?"

"Uh, Ted—" Gibson called out from the edge of the crowd. "I think that about wraps it up. If you don't mind."

Spindler ignored him, keeping his eyes on Kimberly. "Uh, Jack said he thought the plant was unsafe. I think what he wanted to do—"

"That's all, folks," Gibson said, trying to break up the press conference. He fought his way to Spindler and tried to take the big man by the arm.

"One more question," Kimberly said, "you said Godell said the plant was unsafe. Is it? Is that what you, yourself, think? That the plant is unsafe?"

"Uh, it's not my place to say," Spindler said.

"It's not your place! Then whose place *is* it, Mr. Spindler?"

"Let's go, Spindler," Gibson urged, pushing the big man the way a tug pushes a barge.

"I said whose place *is* it?" Kimberly insisted, her voice loud, tears welling in her eyes.

"Wait a minute—" Spindler resisted Gibson's tugging.

"Jack Godell," he said, "was my best friend. And I don't like it that he's going to be marked down as some kind of a nut case, a lunatic. He wasn't a lunatic at all. As a matter of fact, he was the sanest guy I ever met."

"Then you believe," Kimberly's voice broke but she recovered quickly. "He had reason to do what he did tonight? Mr. Spindler, do you believe that he had cause to do what he did? To take over this plant."

Spindler shook his head uneasily like a great bear surrounded by a pack of hounds. "I know this: he wouldn't have done what he did unless he had some kind of a reason. Jack was not that kind of a guy. He didn't go off half-cocked. I don't know all the particulars but I know a few things he told me. But I'm sure there's going to be a big investigation, and I'm sure this time the truth will come out. And when it does, people will know that my friend, Jack Godell was a hero and not some kind of a nut." He closed his mouth with a snap.

"I've said too much already," Spindler murmured, "I've got to go."

Kimberly turned and looked into the camera. The tears on her face were uncontrollable now, but she didn't care. "Pete," she said, fighting for control, "there's still a lot of confusion out here at Ventana. One man is dead. The officials are going back inside and of course, an investigation will begin. I knew Jack Godell only slightly. He was—well, what I could say would be considered biased, so I'll turn it back to you in the studio." When she gave up the mike, Richard was waiting. Sobbing openly, she fell into his arms.

On the monitor back in the studio, Pete Martin came back on camera, smiling as always. "Thank you, Kimberly Wells. We'll be back with more on the Ventana Nuclear Plant take-over by one of its employees, right after this . . ."

Jacovich, looking at the monitor, spoke to one of his aides. "Hell of a job. Didn't I always tell you, that kid could do a hell of a job?"

ABOUT THE AUTHOR

BURTON WOHL was born in New York City and attended Hofstra University. For quite a few years, before turning to novel writing exclusively, Mr. Wohl worked as a journalist both in the United States and abroad, for *The New York Times*, Time-Life, Inc., and other publications. His previous books include: *A Cold Wind in August, The Jet Set, High Encounter*, and four novels based on screenplays, *Posse, That Certain Summer, Mahogany*, and *Casey's Shadow.* His most recent novel is *Soldier in Paradise.*